Folk Tales from China

First Series

SEAGULL PUBLISHING COMPANY
HONG KONG

Contents

THE FROG RIDER	5
THE WOODEN HORSE	29
MA LIANG AND HIS MAGIC BRUSH	53
THE STORY OF HERO SHIGAR	66
THE THIRD SON AND THE MAGISTRATE	77
THE FROG WHO BECAME AN EMPEROR	90
OLIVE LAKE	99
HOW THE BROTHERS DIVIDED THEIR PROPERTY	107
STORIES ABOUT NASRDIN AVANTI	117

The Frog Rider

(A Tibetan Story)

Once upon a time, there lived a poor couple on a far-away high mountain. They grew *chingko* and potatoes on an arid terrace on the mountain-side. They led a hard life.

They were growing old and gradually losing their strength; both longed for a child. They said to each other: "How wonderful it would be if we had a child. Then when we grow old we will have someone to plough our land, to do our allotted task for the *Chungpon** and to chop our firewood so that when we are very old, we two may rest our bent backs a little while sitting at our own *grora*."**

---

* A local district official, with magisterial powers, responsible for the collection of taxes and administration of civil affairs.

** Tibetan homes, both skin tents and stone houses, have a round fire pit in the middle of the floor; an iron grid is placed across it for cooking.

So they both prayed piously to the God of Mountains and Rivers. And soon the wife knew she was going to have a child. Seven months later, she gave birth. But she had a frog, with two big bulging eyes, not a human baby.

The old man said: "What an astonishing thing! This is no baby, but a frog with two bulging eyes. Let us throw him out."

The wife did not have the heart to do such a thing, and replied: "God was not benevolent to us. He gave us a frog instead of a human baby. But anyway this frog was born to us, so don't let us throw him out. Frogs make their home in muddy pools. Put him in the one behind our house, and let him live there."

The old man picked up the Frog, but just as he was carrying him away, the Frog spoke: "Oh Father and Mother! Please don't put me into the pool. I was born to a human being, so let me grow up with human beings. When I grow up I will change the face of our land and change the life of the poor."

The old man was startled and exclaimed: "Wife, what queer happenings! He speaks like a human!"

"But what he said would be good," replied his wife. "It's high time things were changed for us poor people; we just can't go on like this. He cannot be an ordinary frog, if he can speak. Let him stay with us."

They were a kind-hearted couple and the Frog lived with them as though he were really their human child.

Three years went by, when one day the Frog, who had seen how hard and industriously the two old people worked every day, said to the old woman: "Mother, make me a loaf of steamed bread with coarse flour, and put it in a bag for me tomorrow. I am going to the *Chungpon* who lives at the mouth of the valley in the castle with stone towers to ask for the hand of one of his daughters. He has three lovely daughters. I will marry the one who is kind-hearted and capable and bring her home to help you with your daily toil."

"My dear son, don't make such jokes," said the old woman. "As if anyone would give his daughter in marriage to such a small and ugly thing like you! A mere frog, who could be trampled on without a thought!"

"Make me the steamed bread, Mother," said the Frog. "He will consent."

The old woman finally agreed. "Very well, I'll make one for you," she said. "But supposing his household just pour ash on your head when they see you, as people do with monsters?"

"Nay, Mother," said the Frog. "They will not dare to do that."

So the old woman made a big steamed loaf with coarse flour the next morning and put it in a bag.

The Frog hung the bag on his back, and hopped to the *Chungpon's* towered castle at the mouth of the valley.

When he got to the gate, the Frog called out, "Oh, *Chungpon, Chungpon,* open the door."

The *Chungpon* heard someone calling and sent his servant to see who was there.

The servant returned, a surprised look on his face. "How strange! It is nothing but a frog, Master, a very small frog, calling at the gate."

The *Chungpon's* steward said, in the voice of one who always knows what to do, "*Chungpon,* it must be a monster. Let us throw ash on him."

The *Chungpon* disagreed. "No, wait a bit. It may not be a monster," he said. "Frogs usually stay in water. Maybe this one comes on some mission from the Dragon King's palace. Sprinkle milk on him as you would do to a god, and then I will see him for myself."

His servants did as they were bid and gave the Frog a reception as if he were a god. They sprinkled milk on him and cast some into the air.

Then the *Chungpon* went himself to the gate and asked, "Froggy, do you come from the Dragon King's palace? What do you want?"

"I do not come from the Dragon King," answered the Frog. "I have come of my own accord, because your three daughters have all reached marriageable age and I want one for a wife. I come as a suitor. Please give your consent for me to marry one of them."

The *Chungpon* and his servants were all horrified, and the *Chungpon* said, "You are talking nonsense, Frog. You, so small and ugly! How can you be matched with my daughter? Why, many highly-placed *Chungpons* have asked for my daughters' hands and I refused them. Why, then, should I give a daughter of mine to a frog? You are being absurd."

"Oho! That means you don't agree, then," said the Frog. "Very well. If you don't give your consent, I'll laugh."

The *Chungpon* was furious when he heard this. "Frog, you are crazy. If you want to laugh, go ahead."

So the Frog began to laugh. The noise of his laughter was ten times, even a hundred times, louder than a pondful of frogs at night. When he laughed the earth quivered. The high towers of the

Chungpon's castle shook as though they would collapse. Cracks appeared in the walls. Pebbles and dust danced in the air, and the sky and sun were darkened. The *Chungpon's* family and servants ran round and round in the great house, bumping into one another, not knowing what they were doing. Some even carried pieces of furniture over their heads as if that would ward off the calamity.

In desperation, the *Chungpon* put his head out of a window and besought the Frog: "Please do not laugh any more, Froggy, otherwise we shall all be killed. I'll tell my eldest daughter to go with you and be your wife."

The Frog stopped his laughter. Gradually the earth ceased to quiver and the house became stable again.

It was fear which forced the *Chungpon* to give his eldest daughter to the Frog. He ordered his servants to bring out two horses: one for her to ride, and the other to carry her dowry.

The eldest daughter was very unwilling to be married to a frog. She spied two millstones under the eaves as she mounted the horse and secretly took the upper millstone and concealed it in her breast.

The Frog hopped ahead to lead the way and the eldest daughter followed on horseback. All the time she urged her horse to go faster, hoping she would catch up with the Frog and kill him with her horse's hoofs. But the Frog hopped now to the left and now to the right, so that she could not do this. In the end she got so impatient that once when she was very close to the Frog she snatched the millstone out of her breast, threw it at the leaping Frog, and turned to gallop back home.

She had hardly gone any distance when the Frog called out to her, "Stop, Maiden! I have something to say to you." She turned her head and saw the Frog who she hoped had been crushed. He had escaped through the hole in the middle of the mill-stone.

She was startled and pulled her horse up short. The Frog said to her: "We are not destined for each other. Go home, since that is what you want." And he took the horse's bridle, and led her back home.

When they arrived at her father's castle, the Frog said to the *Chungpon*, "We are not suited to each other, so I have brought her back. Give me another one of your daughters, who may be destined for me."

"What a conceited frog you are—you do not know your place!" cried the *Chungpon* in a fury. "Since you bring my daughter back, I'll not give you an-other. What, should I, a *Chungpon*, let you pick and choose among my daughters?" He was trem-bling with rage.

"I suppose you mean you don't agree, then," said the Frog. "Very well, if you don't agree I'll cry."

The *Chungpon* thought to himself that it wouldn't matter if he did cry. It wouldn't be as dangerous as his laughter. So he said, ill-humouredly, "Cry then. Nobody will be afraid because you cry."

So the Frog cried. His wailing sounded like the rain in a summer night. As soon as he started to cry, the sky became black. Thunder rolled all around, and floods poured down the mountain-sides. The land was swiftly turned into seas; the waters kept rising, and flooded the castle and the stone towers. The *Chungpon* and his household climbed up on to the flat roof and huddled there.

The water was rising right up to the parapet. The *Chungpon* had to stretch out his neck over the edge as he cried out to the Frog. "Stop crying, Frog, otherwise we shall all be dead. I'll give my second daughter to you."

The Frog stopped crying immediately and the waters ebbed slowly away.

The *Chungpon* gave orders again to bring out two horses—one to carry his second daughter and the other to carry her dowry, and he bade his second daughter go with the Frog.

The second daughter was also unwilling to go. She took the other millstone when she mounted the horse, and hid it in her breast. On the way, she also tried to make her horse trample on the Frog. And she also hurled the millstone at the Frog and turned to go.

But the Frog called her back. "Maiden, we are not destined for each other," he said. "You may go home." And he took the horse's bridle and led her back.

The Frog gave the second daughter back to the *Chungpon* and asked for the youngest daughter.

This time the *Chungpon* was beside himself with rage. He said, nearly choking, "You sent back my eldest daughter and I gave you my second. You then sent her back. Now you want my third daughter. You are really too exacting. There lives no *Chungpon* in the whole world who could stand this. You . . . you . . . you really have no regard for law and the order of things." He was so carried away with fury that his words stuck in his throat, and he could say no more. No one had ever had to suffer, he felt, as he was suffering then.

The Frog replied calmly, "Why do you grow so angry, *Chungpon*? Your two elder daughters were unwilling to go with me, so I sent them back. But your third daughter is willing. Why, then, should she not come with me?"

"No, no, no!" said the *Chungpon,* hatred in his voice. "She is not willing. No girl is willing to marry a frog. I've let you have your way for the last time."

"You refuse to consent, then?" said the Frog. "If you don't grant my request, I'll hop."

The *Chungpon* was terrified really, but in his overwhelming rage, he shouted, "You may hop if you like. I'll no longer be a *Chungpon* if I'm afraid of your hopping."

So the Frog hopped. When he hopped, the earth vibrated and bobbed up and down like a wave in a tempestuous sea. The mountains around shook so violently that they knocked against one another, until rocks and sand flew into the sky and blacked out the sun. Even the stones and the towers of the *Chungpon's* castle shook so much that it seemed they were going to topple over at any moment.

So the *Chungpon* had to stand up among the ashes and promise to give him the hand of his third daughter. The Frog ceased to hop. The earth and the mountains regained their tranquillity.

The *Chungpon* was forced to send his third daughter riding away with another horse carrying her dowry.

The third daughter, unlike her two sisters, was kind-hearted. She thought that the Frog must be a clever frog and she was willing to go with him.

So the Frog took her home. The mother was amazed when she received them at the door. "Fancy my small and ugly child getting such a beautiful wife," she thought.

The girl was full of industry and used to go out working with the mother on the land. Therefore the old woman loved her, and was respected in return. The mother was very happy.

It became the season of autumn. In those parts it was customary to hold a great horse race every year. Rich and poor for hundreds of *li* around came in with their round skin tents and their newly harvested grain. They burned incense-bearing branches in honour of the gods, danced, drank wine

and raced. The young people used to choose their lovers there. This year the mother wanted the Frog to come with her but he refused. "I won't go, Mother. There are endless mountains to climb. It is too far for me." And he stayed at home, while the others went off.

There were seven days of the festival. The last three days were given over to the horse racing. At the end of each day the winners in the race were surrounded by dancing young girls, and invited to the tents of the girls' fathers, mothers, and brothers to drink the fermented *chingko* wine which the girls brewed in great earthenware jars.

On the third day of the horse races, when the last race was just going to start, a young man dressed all in green came riding in on a green horse, and entered the race course. He was strongly built and handsome. His clothes were made of the best brocades and silk. His saddle was inlaid with silver and gold and rubies. His gun, mounted with silver and coral, swung on his shoulder. Everyone there stared at him as he asked permission to take part in the last race. When the race began he seemed to be in no hurry, but only started to adjust his saddle, even when the other young riders had begun to gallop. But he immediately caught up with them.

All the other riders bent all their attention to the race, as they galloped across the vast meadow, but the young man, even as he rode, loaded his gun and shot down three fluttering eagles which were circling overhead, each one with one shot, from horseback. As he rode past the onlookers, he jumped down from the left of his horse, picked up the most beautiful golden flowers, tossed them to the people on his left, and then jumped down from the right, picked some silver flowers and tossed them to the people on the right. On he rode again. As his horse sped across the green meadow only his horse's hoofs could be seen churning up the turfs, so that it looked as though he were riding the very clouds. The people stood spellbound. He passed all the other riders and was the first at the winning post.

Everyone at the race course was fascinated—old men and women, the praying lamas and the young girls. A whisper ran round the crowd: "Where does he come from? What is his name?"

"He fired from horseback, and jumped down from the left for golden flowers and from the right for silver flowers. Never before has such a sight been seen!"

"What a strong, what a handsome young man! See how his splendid saddle, his horse, his silk and brocades match with him!"

"But where is the girl who can be matched with such a strong and handsome young man?"

All the young girls surrounded the victor, and sang and danced merrily around him, and invited him to their tents to drink the fermented *chingko* wine they had brewed in the great earthenware jars.

But when it was sunset, the young man quickly leaped on his horse and rode away, with never even a word of farewell, in the direction from where the Frog's bride and her parents-in-law came from.

All the people looked after the dust raised by the hoofs of the green horse.

The Frog's bride wondered where the young rider had come from, and she too thought how handsome and strong he was. She too would like to know his name and why he had to go so hurriedly when the

sun set. Perhaps, she thought, he lives very far away. And when she went home, she, like the others, was still puzzled.

The Frog met them at the door. They all began to tell him about the horse race; and were surprised to find he knew all about the happenings, and even about the unknown young rider, before they told him anything.

Next year, come autumn, the annual race was held again, at the same place. The father, the mother and the girl went again.

When the time came for the horse racing, all the people were thinking of the green-costumed rider and his green horse. This year, many said, "We must find out his name, and where he lives, and which *Chungpon* he lives under, if he comes this time."

On the last day, when they were starting the final race, the rider in the green costume, and on his green horse, entered the racing ground as suddenly as if he had descended from heaven. Again he had his beautiful gun with him, but he was wearing an even more gorgeous brocade costume this time. He sat down and drank tea, when all the other riders had started the race! Then he mounted his horse, and as he was galloping swiftly, he again loaded his gun as last year and shot down three eagles. He jumped down from the left and picked up the golden flowers to toss to the people on his left, and jumped down from the right and picked some silver flowers to toss to the people on the right when he rode past them. Then he rode on, as fast as though he were riding a cloud. Nothing but a green cloud flashing across the meadow could be seen. Again he was first past the final post.

The young girls sang and danced to all the quick riders as always. But they danced and sang with special enthusiasm to this young man, and invited him specially to their tents to drink the fermented *chingko* wine they brewed in the great earthenware jars. Then, when the sun was setting, again he sped away, before he could bid them farewell.

The old men and women, the lamas, and the sentimental girls again stared amazedly at the dust raised by his horse's hoofs, and a veritable hubbub arose when they again asked one another who he could be and whence he came. But still this year they omitted to ask him, before he went!

When the old couple and the girl came back home they found that, sure enough, the Frog knew everything that had happened, and how the young man was the victor even though he had started late.

The girl was amazed. How can he know everything, she wondered, if he were not there? Why does the young man have to go before sunset? And why does he ride off in the same direction as us? Can there really be such a good rider in the human world? And what a handsome, strong, and engaging young man he is! Then and there she decided to get to the bottom of it. It seemed only the twinkling of an eye before it was time for the annual race again. The girl went as usual with the parents to burn the branches, dance and drink wine. But on the last day, the day of the great race, the girl said to the mother, "Mother, I don't feel well. My head is as heavy as if it weighed a thousand pounds. I want to go home. Let me take the mule and go, now." The parents were always very considerate to her and let her go back on the mule which carried their tent. Directly she was out of sight of her parents, she urged the mule towards home at a quick trot. When she got there, the first thing she did was to look for the Frog. But she couldn't find him anywhere. And then, by the *grora* she found an empty frog skin, which looked just like her husband's. She picked it up and shed tears of joy, and cried out, "Yes, he *is* the frog rider! Oh God, how happy I am! To have a husband who is such a handsome and strong young man, and such a wonderful rider. Now I don't feel that I shall ever be a match for him! What a happy girl I am!— Yet at the same time what a poor girl I am!"

She kept wiping her tears away, but they still streamed down. She looked again and again at the frog skin, and said, resentfully: "Oh, why must you wear such a hideous skin? Why must you be so small and ugly? Aren't I good enough? Would you rather be a frog, so as not to be my true husband?"

She felt such hatred towards the skin that she decided to burn it. Otherwise, she thought, when he comes back he'll just change again into being a small, horrid frog. So she set to, and burned it.

The sun was sinking when she burned the skin. And suddenly the young man came galloping along on his horse, like a green cloud descending from the sky. He turned pale with horror when he saw her burning the skin, and leaped off his horse to try and snatch the skin from the fire. Too late: only one leg was left.

He heaved a deep sigh and collapsed limply on a big stone in front of the house.

The girl was frightened, and ran to help him into the house.

"My husband," she said sadly, "you're such a fine young man really, and such a good rider. Why do you want to be a frog? Other girls have humans for a husband, but my husband is a frog! Don't you know how unhappy it makes me feel?"

The young man replied: "Lass, you were too impatient. What you did, you did too early. You should have waited till I had enough strength, and then we could have lived happily together. Now I shall not live and the people will not have happiness."

"Have I done wrong, then?" asked the girl. "What shall I do now?"

"It is not your fault. I was too careless," said the young man. "I wanted to try my strength. That was why I went to the contest. But now, neither the people nor we ourselves can be happy. I am not an ordinary human, but the son of Mother Earth. If I could have grown strong enough I would have been able to stand up and work for the people. I want to see a world where the poor are no longer trampled on by the rich, and where common people are not oppressed by officials. I want to see some way by which we can go easily to wonderful Peking and trade our cattle for grain with our brothers, the Hans. But I'm not old enough yet, and have not reached my full strength. I still cannot pass through the cold night without my frog skin and I shall die before daybreak. It would have been warm enough here if I could have grown to full strength, and could have done my work for the people. Then our lives would be comfortable and I could have lived without my frog skin. But it is still too early. I can't stay here on earth. I must go back to my mother, tonight."

Tears welled up in the girl's eyes when she heard this. She clasped the frail body of the young man in her arms, and said, heart-broken, "Oh my husband, you mustn't die! You must, you must live. I won't believe that you can't live."

The girl cried so piteously that, at last, he took her hand in his weak hand and said, "My young wife, don't grieve so. If you really want me to live, there *is* still something you can do." He pointed to the west. "But this can only be done if it is God's will and with his permission. Get on my horse immediately: there is still time, because my horse is so swift-footed. He will carry you to the west, where a celestial hall stands among red clouds. Go in there and appeal to God. Entreat him for these three things, in the name of the happiness of the people. Ask him to promise it before daybreak: Remember, the first is that the people will no longer be divided into rich and poor, the second is that the common people shall not be oppressed by officials, and the third is that there will be some way by which we can go to Peking and have a market there for our cattle and sheep, and buy the five staples from our brothers, the Hans. If God will promise this, we shall have a warm and comfortable life and I shall be able to live without my frog skin even during the night. And then I shall not have to die."

The girl leaped on the horse immediately, and galloped off. It seemed that she was flying in the sky. The wind whistled past her, and she overtook the flashing white clouds. Finally she came to the celestial palace, gleaming rosy-gold like the sun. She went in, and made her appeal to the God. God was moved by her sincerity and granted her requests.

God said to her, "Because you are sincere, I will grant all your requests. But, before the day breaks, you must go to all the houses to tell the people the news. The requests will only be fulfilled if all the people hear before dawn. And it will no longer be cold in these parts, and your husband will be able to pass the night without his frog skin."

The girl rejoiced. She thanked the God, mounted her horse without delay and turned homewards to spread the news to every family before daybreak.

But when she entered the valley, her father, the *Chungpon*, was standing at the gate of their castle.

When he saw his daughter galloping, he exclaimed: "Why, daughter, has something happened? Why are you out riding at this late hour?"

"Oh Father, indeed something has happened!" the girl replied. "God has promised me a wonderful thing. I'm going now to every house, to tell all the people."

"What's the hurry? Stop and tell me what God has promised you," said the *Chungpon.*

"Father, there's no time to stop and tell you," replied the girl. "I'll tell you later."

"That won't do," said her father. "I'm the *Chungpon,* aren't I? You must tell me first." And he strode down the steps and took hold of her horse's reins.

The girl knew she must be rid of him quickly, so she told him everything. "God promised us three things," she began. "The first thing is that there will be no difference between rich and poor."

The *Chungpon* knitted his brows and bawled. "If there is no difference between rich and poor, there will be no distinction in rank among men. How shall your sisters have dowries, then?" He took hold more firmly of the reins.

"The next thing is that the common people will not be oppressed by the officials."

"Not oppressed by the officials, indeed! Then who will do the work for us? Who will tend our cattle and sheep? Who will plough our land?" He nearly choked, then he demanded what the third promise could be.

"That there will be some way by which we can go to Peking to sell our cattle and sheep to our brother Hans, and buy the five staples from them. Oh, Father, when all this comes true it will be lovely and warm here, so that. . . ."

But the *Chungpon* wouldn't hear the end. "This is all nonsense," he bawled. "We are doing quite well with our cattle and sheep now. Why must we have our staples from the Hans? These are certainly not the God's orders. I don't believe a word of it. I'll not let you tell such things to the people."

"I can't stay here any longer, Father," the girl cried. "Let me go!" She tried to ride off, but her father would not let go the reins. The poor girl was beside herself with anxiety, and argued frantically with him.

Just then the cock crowed. The girl jumped and tried to spur the horse away. But the *Chungpon* still held him fast. The *Chungpon*, panting, cried out against his daughter: "Are you crazy? Do you want your sisters to marry without dowries? Do you want to degrade your father, and make him do his own work? Who's going to herd the cattle and sheep? Who'll plough the land? Are you crazy?"

The girl didn't know what to do. The cock crowed a second time, and there she was, still struggling with the *Chungpon*.

Desperate, she whipped her horse hard. The horse reared up in the air, throwing the *Chungpon* to the ground. She had only reached the first house in the valley when the cock crowed for the third time. Dawn was brightening the sky already, and only a few families had heard the promises of God.

The girl's heart sank. Dawn, and she had not succeeded! It was too late. All she could do was to hurry home.

She found the two old people weeping beside the poor young man, and her mother-in-law saying the prayers for the dead.

So it was all in vain! She fell on the body of her beloved young man and wept bitterly, blaming her father and herself.

The frog rider's body was buried on a cliff halfway up the mountain. And every evening at dusk the girl wept beside his grave, until one day, she turned into a stone. No longer could her weeping be heard.

The stone still stands there beside the grave. From a distance you can see it is like a girl praying, with her long hair flowing over her shoulders. She prays for ever at her husband's grave.

Translated by Yu Fan-chin
Illustrations by Chang Kuang-yu

The Wooden Horse

(A Uighur Story)

One day, a carpenter and a blacksmith started to argue.

"I am more skilled than you!" said the carpenter.

"How can you say such a thing? I am a far better craftsman than you!" said the blacksmith.

They argued on and on without reaching any conclusion. In the end they agreed to go and ask the King to decide the matter for them.

On seeing them, the King asked, "What have you come for?"

"I am a carpenter," said one, "and there's no other carpenter in the world who can make such ingenious things as I do. But this blacksmith claims to be a better craftsman than I."

"Everyone who sees my work is full of praise," said the other. "Yet he insists that I am not so skilled as he!"

And they begged in one voice, "Your Majesty, we ask you to judge between us. Please say which of us is the better craftsman."

But the King also found himself in a quandary. "How are we to judge of such a matter? We have never even seen your work! Go back and make something, and bring it here in ten days from now."

So the two went back, each to his own work. Ten days later they again appeared before the King. The blacksmith had brought a big fish of wrought iron.

"What use is that?" asked the King.

"This fish of mine can swim in the sea even when loaded with a hundred thousand bags of grain."

The King could barely suppress his mirth. This stupid fellow is doomed to failure, he thought. So much iron and yet he claims it can swim? However, he called on his men to load it with a hundred thousand bags of grain and put it in the sea. "See if it will swim!" he said.

Strange to say, the fish swam adroitly and swiftly. Everyone was amazed and delighted. The King praised the blacksmith highly. "We will make you an official," he said. And he thereupon appointed him the head of a street.

The carpenter had made a wooden horse. When the King saw it he looked disappointed. "Surely this is a toy for children?" he asked. "How can you think of comparing it with the fish?"

"Indeed, it is far superior to the fish!" answered the carpenter. "Do you see these twenty-six keys? Turn the first one and the horse will fly. Turn another and it will fly faster. When the twenty-sixth is turned, it will go faster than any bird. In fact, you can easily take a trip around the world on this horse."

As he was talking, the youngest son of the King happened to come by. The very mention of a horse that could fly aroused his curiosity. How wonderful it would be to fly up into the sky and see the world from there! He begged his father to let him try the horse.

"Certainly not!" said the King. "How can you know whether it will really fly? What if it falls down to earth?"

"Don't worry, it cannot fall," the carpenter hastened to assure him.

The young Prince continued to plead with his father. He was his father's favourite son, and the King had never before refused him anything he had asked. Finally the King said, "Very well, you may try. But ride slowly, and don't turn any of the keys except the first."

The young Prince promised. He mounted the horse and turned the first key. The horse really flew. From on high, the Prince looked down upon the mountains and rivers, the trees, cities and people. Everything was far below him, and the higher he flew the further they all receded. He was tremendously exhilarated. One after another, he turned the rest of the keys. The horse flew faster and faster. In no time all the people, the trees and even the cities vanished from sight.

He had flown a long way when he began to feel hungry. Fortunately, he saw a city immediately below him. He tightened the keys. The wooden horse slowed down and landed safely. After having a good meal he put up at an inn. He was overjoyed by his journey, for in such a short time it had brought him to a new city, one that he had never seen before.

The next day he went sightseeing in the streets. A few turns brought him to a square where he saw a crowd of people standing there, gazing into the sky. "There must be something very strange up there," he thought. So walking across to where they stood, he also gazed upwards, only to find there was nothing to see.

"What are you all looking at?" he asked a man standing by him.

The man looked at him closely and then explained. "The King of our country has a daughter," he said. "She is so beautiful, it would be impossible to find any other girl in the world to match her. The King loves her to distraction and won't allow anyone else to set eyes on her. While she was living in his palace, he hardly knew a moment's peace. So he built a palace for her high in the sky. She lives there entirely on her own. Every day, when his duties are finished, the King goes to see her. He has been there for some time now and will soon come back. These people are waiting for him."

All this sounded extremely strange to the Prince. "How is it possible to build a palace in the sky?" he asked.

"It was built by a god. Only the King can go there."

The young Prince could not get this strange story out of his mind. That night, he mounted his wooden horse and rode up into the sky. Sure enough, there was a large palace there. Dismounting at the door, he walked in.

When the Princess saw someone enter, she thought it must be her father. On seeing her mistake, she decided the visitor was a god, for no human being could possibly have come. So she stood up to welcome him.

To the young Prince, she seemed as beautiful as a goddess, and he fell in love with her at first sight.

"I should be the happiest man on earth if I could have a wife like her," he thought.

At the same time the Princess was casting admiring glances at the young and handsome Prince. Love stirred in her heart. "Why should my father lock me up in a place like this where I cannot see anyone?"

she complained to herself. "I also want someone to love me, to caress me."

Without knowing quite how it came about, they embraced each other.

At daybreak the young Prince flew back to the inn. Shortly afterwards the King went to the heavenly palace to see his daughter.

Now every time the King visited the Princess he used to weigh her, for he knew that once a woman had associated with a man, she would put on weight. That day, to his great surprise, he found the Princess was two catties heavier. His eyes flashed fire and his beard bristled with rage. "There is certainly some reason for this!" he thought. He returned at once to his palace to discover what it might be.

When they saw him so unhappy, his ministers came to ask what was the matter. He told them all about it. "Who could go up there except myself?" he said. "Please think of some way of catching this person."

"We have four knights," said the ministers. "Your Majesty can take them up and place them at the four corners of the palace. If the man tries again, he is sure to be captured."

The King thought this was a good idea. When night came, he escorted the four knights to the heavenly palace, and, giving each his place, told them to keep watch. When everything was properly arranged, he returned to earth.

Who could have guessed, however, that the knights were such heavy sleepers that they would stand and sleep at their posts? The young Prince spent the night there again. When the King weighed the Princess the next day, she was eight catties heavier than before. The King was speechless with anger.

By then the matter had become the talk of the town. The King was so ashamed that he refused to appear in public. He called in one of his ministers and asked for his advice. The minister suggested that he should smear the Princess' bed and chairs with wet paint. "Then tomorrow," he said, "we may search the city for the one who has paint on him. The wrongdoer will hardly be able to escape!"

The King accepted the suggestion. He put paint on the bed, the chairs and every piece of furniture. That night, the young Prince went there again. On his way back to the city, he found paint all over his clothes. He immediately took them off and threw them away. Although the clothes were studded with jewels, he did not regret them. For are not jewels of small consequence to one who is in love?

There lived in the city a poor old man, who rose every morning before dawn to knock people up for morning prayers. That day, he was on his rounds when he saw something fall from the sky. Clothes of the finest quality! "It is certainly God who has sent me these," he thought. "Probably because I have been serving Him all my life." He took the clothes home.

In the evening the whole city went to the service in the temple. Among them was a man sent by the King. The old man had gladly put on the clothes given him by God, not knowing of the great misfortune that lay in store for him. Even as he was praying, he was arrested.

"How did your clothes get marked with paint?" demanded the King.

"They were like this when I picked them up in the street."

The King did not believe him. He sent him to prison, where he was convicted on a confession extracted from him by torture. He was then bound and sent to the square to be hanged.

This was no small event in the city. People had been wondering what sort of man the Princess' lover could be. When they saw this old man with the rope round his neck, they could not believe their eyes. The whole city was talking about the case and all thought the old man had been wronged.

The gossip came to the ears of the young Prince. Feeling sorry for the old man, he rushed to the square with the wooden horse under his arm. There was the old man already on the rope. "Don't hang him!" shouted the Prince. "He isn't guilty! I am the one who went to the heavenly palace and stayed with the Princess. The clothes with the paint on are mine. If you like, you may kill me, but set him free immediately."

The executioner stayed his hand and sent a messenger to the King. "A young man has declared himself guilty," ran the message. "Tell us which one to hang."

"Hang the young man who has confessed!" ordered the King.

The executioners released the old man. But as they advanced towards the young Prince, meaning to bind him, he jumped on his horse, turned the keys and flew off, leaving the executioners stupefied. When the King saw so many of his men outwitted by a mere stripling of a boy, he showed all the symptoms of an apoplectic stroke.

The young Prince went to the heavenly palace and said to the Princess, "Our love is becoming dearer with every passing day. To think of parting with each other is out of the question. Since your father has discovered our secret, he will not allow me to live in the city. There is only one way out: come with me to my father's place. He is sure to like you."

To this the Princess replied, "I have made up my mind to stay with you always. Wherever you go, I will go!"

They hurried out of the heavenly palace and flew away on the wooden horse. They had flown a long way when the Princess cried: "I have forgotten the two jewels Mother gave me when I was a child. She told me I should present them to my husband's parents on my wedding day. I forgot to bring them with me. How can I go without them?"

"We are so far from the palace now," said the Prince. "Don't bother about them."

"No, no! I cannot go without the jewels. I shall make myself a laughing-stock if I have no presents to give your parents when I see them."

The young Prince could not but fall in with her wishes. He turned the keys tight and the horse landed. "I shall wait for you here," he said. "Take the horse, go quickly and get the jewels, and return as soon as you can."

The Princess mounted and flew off.

You will recall that the King had collapsed when he saw the Prince fly off into the sky. The first thing he thought of when his ministers restored him to consciousness was his daughter. He hurried to the heavenly palace, only to find the Princess gone. As he was wondering what to do, he saw her returning. He hid himself behind the bed. The moment she came into the room, he jumped out and caught her. He took her back to his palace and shut her in an empty room. The wooden horse had also fallen into his hands. Not knowing how to use it, he threw it into another empty room.

Some time before, there had been another king who, having heard about the beauty of the Princess, asked someone to speak to her father, proposing a marriage between her and his son. The King had refused. Now that the Princess had involved herself in scandal, however, none of the noblemen nearby would ask for her hand. So the King was thinking of marrying her to a distant place. He wrote a letter to the king who had made the proposal, saying, "As my daughter is now of an age to marry, I am willing to marry her to your son. From now on we shall be relatives and our two countries will for ever maintain friendly relations. I hope your son will come for the wedding and take her back with him after it."

How the King dealt with his daughter will not be described here. We will learn instead how the Prince fared while waiting for his sweetheart. He waited for her for a long time. Looking around he found himself in a vast desert, surrounded by high dunes. As the wind blew, the sands shifted to and fro. The sun beat down upon him and there was not a blade of grass to be seen. He was hungry and thirsty, and craved for water. But search as he might, he could not find a drop. Hoping he might be able to see something from the top of one of the dunes, he tried climbing. With each step he took his feet sank into the sand, and it was only after an arduous climb that he managed to reach the top. As he raised his head to look around, the sand beneath his feet started to slide down the dune like ice melting in spring. Steadying himself, he saw a prosperous-looking orchard before him. There were all varieties of trees, laden with ripe fruit—red and green, clustered thickly on the branches. It looked very appetizing. Running into the orchard, he picked and ate a few peaches. They were sweet and fragrant and the juice trickled from his mouth. He was no longer hungry. Leaning against a tree, he fell asleep.

When he woke up and wiped his face with his hand, he found he had grown a thick beard and whiskers. He could not imagine what had happened. He had never had a beard before. He pondered over the matter for a long time until he felt hungry again. This time he did not dare to touch the peaches, for he had begun to suspect them. He went to a pear-tree, pulled down a branch, and picked some of the fruit. They were big and fresh-flavoured, with thin peel. The more he ate, the more he liked them. When he was finally satisfied, he went to sleep again.

It was almost dark when he awoke. As he stretched himself, his head knocked against the tree trunk, and seemed heavier than usual. Feeling it gingerly, he touched two long, thick horns. His beard had turned snow white and grown a foot long. He dared not imagine what he looked like. "When the Princess comes back, she won't recognize me! She won't love me any more! Oh, whatever shall I do?" The longer he brooded over it, the lower his spirits sank. Unable to restrain his sobs, he cried himself to exhaustion and finally fell asleep.

In his dreams he saw an old man standing before him, who touched his head and said, "Why are you so sad, my son?"

The young Prince poured out the tale of his misfortunes.

"Don't worry," said the old man. "Go and pick up some dried peaches and pears from under the trees and eat them, and your beard, whiskers and horns will all drop off. Go away from here, my son. Don't stay here any longer. There are devils living here. They are sleeping now. If they were awake, they would have devoured you."

The young Prince listened in amazement. Waking from his dream, he rubbed his eyes. The moon was riding high and a cold wind was whistling. The sand no longer felt hot. Just as the old man of his dream had told him, he gathered up a handful of dried peaches, and another of dried pears, and ate them. When he had finished eating, he felt his head and face. The beard, whiskers and horns were all gone. He thought for a moment, then tore down some twigs from a willow and wove them into a basket. He filled it with peaches and pears, both dried and fresh, and hurried away from the orchard.

He wanted to go home but did not know where it was. He decided not to bother about it, but to walk at random. Wherever he went, he was surrounded by desolate sands. He ate the dried peaches and pears when hungry, slept on the ground when tired, and resumed his walk the moment he woke up. Thus seven days and seven nights passed. All the time he had not seen even a bird, let alone a man. At last he found himself on a road. With a sigh of relief, he sat down by the roadside.

The first person to pass by was a man with a donkey. He told the Prince that he could reach home by going east, and get to the Princess' country by going west. "What sense is there in going home after I have lost both the Princess and the wooden horse?" he thought, and so he turned towards the west.

On the way, he was overtaken by a cavalcade of men on horseback. They were well armed and the horses were well equipped. The whole procession looked very grand.

In the middle of the cavalcade was a coach with glass windows, adorned with golden traceries, and drawn by four pedigree horses decked with silks and satins. The young Prince stepped aside to get a better look. Unexpectedly the coach pulled up and a man came over to him to ask what he was selling.

"I have nothing to sell!" he replied.

The man pointed to his basket, saying: "Are they not peaches and pears? Our prince has been travelling all day. He is thirsty and hungry. Please sell us a little fruit."

"They are not for sale, they are my food. Have you seen so much as a single blade of grass on the road? What will I eat if I sell you the fruit?"

The prince in the coach shouted at the man to be quick. Then he sent another man with a piece of gold, saying: "Buy them and pay as much as the boy asks."

At this point the young Prince asked, "Where are you going?"

"Our prince is going to his bride, who is the Princess of the city there." The man pointed towards the west.

The young Prince was taken aback. But hiding his agitation, he asked for further details. He discovered it was no other princess than his sweetheart that the prince in the coach was intending to marry. He accepted the gold, and gave them two of the reddest fresh peaches and two of the biggest fresh pears. The prince was delighted and ate them as quickly as he could.

They moved off, the coach bumping along with the prince sound asleep inside. No sooner had he waked than he began to cry aloud with fright. The ministers ran up to the coach to see what had happened. But the prince had disappeared. Inside the coach was a strange animal with two horns and a face covered with white whiskers and a beard. The procession halted to wait for the boy who had sold them the fruit.

Soon the young Prince came. The ministers stopped him and asked, "What kind of fruit was it that you sold to our prince?"

"Why, I picked it myself!"

"Then why has our prince grown a beard and horns since he ate your fruit?"

Far from being surprised, of course, the young Prince was only too glad to find the other prince in such a state. "But why haven't I grown anything?

And I am eating the fruit every day!" he retorted, concealing his joy.

The ministers could find no words to answer him.

The young Prince pretended to think for a while, then, as though an idea had just dawned upon him, he said, "Did your prince by any chance fall asleep after he had eaten the fruit?"

"Yes, indeed, he did," the ministers nodded.

"Then you can't blame anyone. You have come from other parts, so you wouldn't know there is a maxim to be observed in this place—no sleep after eating. If you fall asleep, you will certainly grow a beard and horns."

On hearing this, the ministers looked at one another in fear and despair. They could only imagine that their prince himself was to blame, for being so greedy and slothful. But what was to be done now?

They talked the matter over. It was clear that the Princess would never marry their prince as he was. "It would be best if we went back at once," said one. "We will only be driven out if we go on." But the prince felt he would sooner die than return home. "I have been thinking of the Princess for so long," he said. "She is mine now, and I will not let her slip out of my hands."

The minister who was most intent upon serving the interests of his king finally thought up a plan.

"Let us find a handsome young man to play the part of the prince," he suggested. "By this ruse, we shall get the Princess. Once she is in our country, she will be helpless."

This won everybody's approval. They started looking around for a handsome young man. Comparing one with another, they came to the conclusion that none was so good-looking as the boy who sold the fruit. They spoke to him about it. The young Prince feigned reluctance. "It has nothing to do with me," he said. "You will have to manage by yourselves. I have my own affairs to take care of."

The ministers kept pressing him to do them the favour, promising him five pieces of gold. "Five isn't enough," said the young Prince. "Then we'll give you seven." So it was settled. They made him sit in the coach, and put the prince with horns on a horse, veiling his face and covering his head with a piece of cloth. They told him to hide in a room after entering the city, and on no account let himself be seen. With these new arrangements, they moved forward.

Upon their arrival, the King came out of the city to welcome them. He was glad to see that his son-in-law was so young and handsome and had come with so many presents. At the same time he was worrying over his daughter's disgrace. If it were known to the Prince, he thought, he would not marry her. So he sped up the preparations. The wedding feast was to last for four days and four nights. It was arranged that the elderly people should be provided with drinks outside, while the young men and women should remain inside, to amuse the Prince and Princess. The King hoped that by keeping the guests busy all day long, they would have no chance to hear about his daughter's lapse.

The celebrations had been going on for three days. All this time the Princess had never once stopped weeping. She would not lift her veil to look at the bridegroom, for her thoughts were with another whom she loved with all her heart. On the fourth day, the uneasy King sent an old and trusted woman to find out whether the Prince loved the Princess.

That night at the banquet in the palace the young Prince, sitting beside the Princess, seized the opportunity when no one was watching them to whisper to her that it was he who had come back. On hearing this, the Princess lifted her veil and peeped at him. She thought she must be dreaming, for what could her father be thinking of in bringing him back to her?

The young Prince was afraid that she might give herself away, so he quietly told her what had happened to him and asked her to act as though she knew nothing about it. After this the Princess dried her tears, talked and laughed, and more than once danced with him. While dancing, they talked over their plans for running away. The young Prince said that after the wedding, when she came to say goodbye to her father, she should ask for the wooden horse, and should refuse to leave without it, no matter how the King should try to intimidate her.

The old woman returned to the King and said, "Words cannot describe how they love each other! They have been dancing and singing together all night." The King was overjoyed.

The next day a great number of nobles gathered at the gates of the palace to see the Princess off. The Prince and his entourage were all ready. But in the palace, the Princess, clasping the King by the leg, demanded the wooden horse and refused to leave without it. The King flew into a rage. He even called in the executioners to frighten her off. Far from being frightened, however, she declared she would rather die than leave without the horse. The King was furious, and at his wit's end. The nobles waiting outside grew impatient. They went in to ask about the delay. "This useless daughter of mine is bothering us with her childish nonsense," said the King. "She insists on taking a wooden horse she used to have."

At this the nobles laughed. "Why not let her have the toy since she is so fond of it?"

The King could no longer object. He brought out the wooden horse and gave it to her. Then the cavalcade moved off.

Many days had passed since they started on their journey. The attendants waited upon the young Prince and Princess with great care. Not for a moment would they leave them alone, thus depriving them of any opportunity to escape. As they neared their destination, the young couple became more and more anxious. At last the young Prince hit upon a ruse and told the Princess about it. When they reached the gates of the palace, he said, she should demand that they present her with seven plates of gold coins to scatter on the ground, to be picked up by anyone who liked. If this was not done, she was to refuse to get down from the coach.

The Princess learned her role by heart, and when the time came, the coins were scattered all over the place. As a result, everyone started scrambling for the gold, like a swarm of bees. By then the young Prince had got the wooden horse ready. He helped the Princess on to it, and turned the keys. The next moment they were up in the sky. They flew towards the young Prince's country and arrived there safe and sound.

The young Prince's father had been thinking of his son day and night since he was lost. He placed the full blame on the carpenter, and wanted to have him executed. Eventually he had him nailed on a bridge, and he was still there three days later when the young Prince returned.

"Father," said the Prince, "the carpenter's horse has been invaluable. Without it I could not have toured so many countries, nor found so lovely a bride. Neither could I have returned to join you again. Please give the carpenter a worthy reward."

The King was filled with remorse. He had to tell the young Prince the truth. At the same time, he sent a man hurrying to the bridge to rescue the victim. The carpenter was still alive, so he was taken down and brought to the King's palace. The young Prince himself looked after him, and, when his wounds were healed, presented him with a large sum of gold.

The young Prince and Princess had another wedding ceremony. Soon he succeeded to the throne.

Translated by Ting Wan-tao
Illustrations by Chang Kuang-yu

Ma Liang and His Magic Brush

(A Story of the Han People)

Once upon a time there was a boy named Ma Liang, whose father and mother had died when he was a child, so that he had to earn his living by gathering firewood and cutting weeds. He was a very clever boy and longed to learn to paint, but he could not afford to buy even one brush.

One day Ma Liang passed a private school while the schoolmaster was painting, and was fascinated to watch the strokes made by his brush. Before he knew it he had slipped into the school.

"I want so much to learn to paint," he said. "Please, will you lend me a brush?"

"What!" The master glared at him. "A little beggar wants to paint? You must be dreaming!" He drove the lad away.

But Ma Liang had a will of his own.

"Why shouldn't I learn to paint even if I am poor?" he said to himself.

He made up his mind to learn, and practised hard every day. When he went up the mountain to gather firewood, he would use a twig to draw birds on the sand; when he went to the river to cut reeds, he would dip his finger into the water and trace fish on the rock; when he got home, he would sketch his few sticks of furniture on the walls of his cave, until soon the four walls were covered with his drawings.

Time passed quickly; and since Ma Liang did not let a single day go by without practising drawing, naturally he made rapid progress. People who saw

his pictures almost expected the birds to warble and the fish to swim—they were so true to life. But still Ma Liang had no brush! He often thought how happy he would be if he could have one.

One night, tired out after working and drawing all day, Ma Liang fell fast asleep as soon as he lay down on his pallet. Then an old man with a long white beard came up to him and gave him a brush.

"This is a magic brush," said the old man. "Use it carefully!"

Ma Liang took the brush in his hand. It was of glittering gold and rather heavy.

"What a beautiful brush!" He jumped for joy. "Thank you ever so much. . . ."

Before Ma Liang could finish thanking him, the old man with the white beard vanished. The lad woke with a start. So it was a dream! But how could it be a dream when the magic brush was there in his hand? He was lost in wonder.

He painted a bird with this magic brush, and the bird flapped its wings, then soared up into the sky where it began to sing merrily for him to hear. He painted a fish with this magic brush, and the fish frisked its tail, then plunged into the river and sported in the water for him to see. He was in raptures.

With this magic brush, Ma Liang painted every day for the poor folk in his village: a plough, a hoe, an oil lamp or a bucket, for whichever family had none.

But no secret can be kept for ever. The news of Ma Liang's magic brush soon reached the ears of a rich landlord in that village; and the landlord sent two of his men to seize Ma Liang and force the boy to paint for him.

Though Ma Liang was only a lad, he had plenty of courage. He had seen through those rich people, and no matter how the landlord threatened or flattered him, he refused to paint a single picture. So

the landlord shut him up in a stable and began to starve him.

Three days later it began to snow heavily, and by the evening snow lay thick on the ground. Thinking that Ma Liang must have died of cold if not of hunger by now, the landlord went to the stable to look. As he approached the door he saw red firelight shining through its chinks and sniffed a delicious smell of food. And peeping through a crack in the door, what should he see but Ma Liang toasting himself by a big stove and eating hot cakes! The landlord could hardly believe his eyes. Where had the stove and cakes come from? Then he realized that Ma Liang must have painted them. Trembling with rage, he summoned his men to kill Ma Liang and seize the magic brush.

But by the time a dozen of his fiercest men rushed into the stable, Ma Liang was nowhere to be seen—all they found was a ladder leaning against the wall by which Ma Liang had made his escape. The landlord lost no time in mounting the ladder in pursuit, but he tumbled and fell before he reached the third rung. And when he got to his feet again, the ladder had vanished.

After escaping from the landlord's house Ma Liang knew he could not hide in the village, for that would only get the friends who sheltered him into trouble.

He must go far away. He waved farewell to the familiar cottages, murmuring:

"Goodbye, dear friends!"

Then he painted a fine horse, mounted it and galloped down the highway.

He had not gone far when he heard a hubbub behind him, and turning his head saw the landlord and nearly a score of his lackeys pursuing him on horseback. They carried bright torches, and a sword flashed in the landlord's hand.

Soon they were quite near. Calmly, Ma Liang drew a bow and an arrow with his magic brush, and fitted the arrow to the bow. "Whiz!" The arrow pierced the landlord's throat and he fell headlong

from his horse. Then Ma Liang lashed his own steed so that it flew forward as if on wings.

Ma Liang galloped down the highway for several days and nights without stopping, till he came to a town and decided to stay there; for he was now far, far away from his native village. Since he could find no work in that town, he had to paint pictures and sell them in the market. But in order that he might not be discovered, he took care not to let his pictures come to life by drawing birds without a beak or animals with one leg missing.

One day, after painting a crane with no eyes, he was careless enough to splash ink on the bird's head where the eyes should have been; whereupon the crane opened its eyes, flapped its wings and flew off. At once the whole town was agog with excitement. And some busybody reported it to the emperor, who sent officers to summon Ma Liang to court. Ma Liang had no wish to go; but with fair promises and veiled threats they carried him off.

Ma Liang had heard many stories about the emperor's cruelty to the poor, and hated him from the bottom of his heart. He was certainly not going to serve such a man. So when the emperor ordered him to paint a dragon, he painted a toad instead; when the emperor ordered him to paint a phoenix, he painted a cock instead. This ugly toad and filthy cock leapt and flapped around the emperor, leaving dirt and droppings everywhere, till the whole palace stank. Then the emperor, in a towering rage, ordered his guards to seize the magic brush from Ma Liang and throw him into prison.

Now that the emperor had this magic brush, he tried painting with it himself. First he painted a gold mountain. Then, thinking one gold mountain was not enough, he added another and yet another, until his picture was a mass of mountains. But when the painting was finished, what do you think happened to those gold mountains? They turned into a pile of rocks. And because they were top-heavy, they toppled down, nearly crushing the emperor's feet in their fall.

Still the emperor was not cured of his greed. Having failed to paint gold mountains, he decided to paint gold bricks. He painted a brick; but it seemed too small. He painted a bigger one; but still it seemed too small. Finally he painted a long, long golden bar. But when the picture was finished, what do you think happened? The golden bar turned into an enormous python, which rushed at him with its huge, crimson mouth wide open; and the emperor fainted for fear. Luckily, his officers were quick in coming to the rescue; otherwise he would have been swallowed by this terrible monster.

Finding he could make no use of the magic brush himself, the emperor released Ma Liang and spoke him fair, presenting him with gold and silver and promising to give him a princess in marriage.

Ma Liang, who had already formed a plan, pretended to agree to all these proposals. Then the emperor was very pleased and returned him the magic brush.

"If he paints a mountain," thought the emperor, "wild beasts may come out of it. Better paint the sea!"

So he ordered Ma Liang to paint the sea first.

Ma Liang took up his magic brush; and, sure enough, a clear, boundless sea appeared before the emperor. Its blue surface was unruffled and it shone like an immense jade mirror.

"Why are there no fish in this sea?" asked the emperor, looking at it.

Ma Liang made a few dots with his magic brush, whereupon fish of all the colours of the rainbow appeared. Frisking their tails, they sported merrily for a while; then swam slowly far out to sea.

The emperor had been watching them with the greatest pleasure; so as they swam further and further away he urged Ma Liang:

"Hurry up and paint a boat! I want to sail out to sea to watch those fish."

Ma Liang painted a huge sailing-boat, upon which the emperor and empress, princes, princesses and many ministers embarked. Then, with a few strokes, he drew wind. Fine ripples appeared on the sea and the boat moved off.

But the emperor found the pace too slow. Standing at the bow, he shouted:

"Let the wind blow harder! Harder!"

A few powerful strokes from Ma Liang's magic brush brought a strong wind. The sea grew rough, and the white sails billowed out as the boat scudded towards mid-ocean.

Ma Liang drew a few more strokes. Then the sea roared, big waves rolled, and the vessel began to keel over.

"That's enough wind!" shouted the emperor at the top of his voice. "Enough, I say!"

But Ma Liang paid no attention. He continued to wield his magic brush. The sea was lashed into fury and billows broke over the deck.

The emperor, drenched through, clung to the mast, shaking his fist at Ma Liang and shouting.

Ma Liang, however, pretended to hear nothing, and went on drawing wind. A hurricane blew black clouds before it to darken the sky; and angry billows reared themselves higher and higher to crash down one after the other on the boat. At last the vessel keeled over, capsized and was shattered. The emperor and his ministers sank to the bottom of the sea.

After the emperor's death, the story of Ma Liang and his magic brush spread far and wide. But what became of Ma Liang? Nobody knows for certain.

Some say that he went back to his native village and rejoined his peasant companions.

Others say that he roamed the earth, painting for the poor wherever he went.

Translated by Tso Cheng
Illustrations by Chang Kuang-yu

The Story of Hero Shigar

(A Story of the Yi People)

Long, long ago, when there were seven suns and six moons in the sky, the whole earth was bright and the weather warm; birds and animals lived prosperously. It was at such a time that Hero Shigar was born, grew up and got married. One day in early spring, Shigar left his two wives and his home on the island in the East Sea, and taking his sword, mounted his flying horse and started to travel over the whole world to see whether everyone — people, birds and animals—was living in peace and equality according to the will of God.

He had been travelling for a long time when one day he came upon a plateau by the Liangshan Mountain where a flock of birds were cawing lugubriously. I have travelled over half the world, thought he, and have seen people, birds and animals living in peace and equality. Why are these birds so sad? So he walked up to them.

"All the other birds and animals on earth live happily and peacefully. What makes you so sad?" he asked.

Shigar's loud voice made all the birds turn to him.

"All birds and animals living in peace?" retorted an eloquent Lark. "This was in the past, Hero. Since an atrocious python emerged from the mountain, our peace has been disturbed."

"What?"

"A python! A python in the East Mountain!" said Lark, his tears streaming down. "It used the light of the six moons to train its thick, stout body by and the heat of the seven suns to make it incomparably strong. It will not seek food for itself, but demands that we offer him one bird a day. If we fail he will kill the entire bird kingdom. It's Partridge's turn today. We're saying goodbye to him."

Shigar was very sorry for Partridge and the other birds. "Why don't you fight with it instead of giving up your lives obediently?" he asked.

When he said this all the birds began to talk at once. Lark's contribution was the most to the point: "Fight? He has no equal! Only when we can get rid of all the suns and moons can we cause the python to change back to his original size, and die of cold."

"All right! I'll get rid of them," said Shigar, turning to go even as he spoke.

He said no further word, but went up to the top of the mountain, drew his bow and began to shoot at the suns. The first one he hit turned into a ball of black smoke and dropped. Then the second, the third, and. . . . When the sixth sun was down the seventh began to speak. "Stop, Shigar!" it said. "If you shoot me down too, the world will have no warmth. Everything on earth will die of cold, including you!"

"You are right," said Shigar thoughtfully. "But mind. From henceforth, you must not shine on evil birds and animals."

The birds raised a joyful clamour as they saw the six suns dropping down one by one.

They flew in great flocks to the python's cave. It was still alive, but was curled up, shivering. The birds discussed the matter for a while, and then sent the Sparrow-Hawk to tell Shigar that if he were to shoot the moons down as well the python would not be able to harm them again.

Shigar set to work without delay. He shot down the first moon, the second and then the third. . . .

When he had done away with five of them the sixth moon began to speak.

"Stop, Shigar! If you shoot me down too, there will be no light on earth. Everything, including you, will be blind."

"All right!" he said, after a minute's thought. "But from henceforth you must not shine on evil birds and animals!"

He came down from the mountain with the Sparrow-Hawk and went back to the plateau where the birds were celebrating the great day. Every kind of bird was to be seen, jostling and rubbing wings, all in great joy. As soon as the Lark and the Partridge saw the flash of Shigar's sword they thanked the Hero in the name of all birds:

"We thank you, Hero Shigar. The python who disturbed the peace has died of cold. Our happy life is restored. Not all the birds on earth could do enough to repay you."

"There is no need to thank me. I wish you happiness for ever," smiled Shigar.

He left the birds and continued on his journey.

He soon came to a walled village. Directly he went through the gate he saw crowds hurrying along the streets. All of them looked anxious and careworn. He reined his horse up at the side of the road and, as he watched, felt grieved himself. Some dreadful calamity must have befallen this village! He dismounted and spoke to an old woman. "Old lady," he said with a bow. "The whole world is living in peace and happiness. Why are you all so grieved here?"

"Living in peace? We did live in peace before. But that was in the past. We have no more peace now! Can you see a single cow or sheep in our village? The grass outside our village has grown knee-high and the water in the spring flows wastefully into the earth! Now it is the turn for human beings to be eaten. Oh, God, why must I see this in my old age?" She groaned and pointed at her white hair.

"What? Is there something disturbing the peace here, too? Peace on earth is the will of God. No one should disturb it!"

Shigar, tall and handsome as he was, had a loud voice. A crowd quickly gathered round him, telling him their sad story.

"A monster emerged from the sea in the west," said one old man. "He has been coming out often to make mischief and has already eaten countless cows and sheep. Now he's become lazy and has ordered us to send his food down to the seashore every day. If we don't he will destroy our village and sink it to the bottom of the sea. . . ." The old man was breathing hard with emotion, and a young one went on.

"He's eaten all the cows and sheep, and now is starting on human beings."

"What sort of beast is this monster?" asked Shigar.

"The wizard says it is a noxious dragon!" someone answered.

Shigar went immediately to find the wizard.

"What do you know about this noxious dragon?" Shigar demanded loudly, as soon as he found the wizard.

"Everything!" the wizard said. He dropped his head and would not meet Shigar's eyes.

"What good are your prayers, then? Aren't you doing anything when you see your people being eaten up?"

"I have prayed my lips numb and my heart weary, Hero. But the dragon is not to be controlled by prayers. When it is in the water it cannot be found. When it is on the land a knife tempered nine times would not injure it at all. It can only be killed by fire. And how can we burn it?"

"There must be a way!"

Shigar bowed his head and pondered. Then he mounted his horse and flew straight towards the east. Soon he reached a big, black, iron mountain where not a single blade of grass grew. He walked three times round the mountain and picked up three iron bars as thick through as a rice bowl and flew back with them. Although it was thousands of miles to go there and back he only spent as long a time as it would take to eat a meal.

Shigar asked the people to gather wood, heat the iron bars red-hot at the seashore, and kill their last sheep. He put the iron bars together in the form of a door-frame, and put the sheep underneath. The smell of the sheep, nicely roasted by the red-hot bars, was carried along by the wind. . . .

Quite quickly a great wind arose and a water-spout over ten foot high shot up in the sea. A black, noxious dragon emerged and rushed straight towards the roasted sheep. But before it could take one mouthful, the three red-hot iron bars crashed down on it. It writhed and shrieked in agony, and steam rushed out of its nostrils. Water flowed out of it in a stream. Soon it was burned to death.

The villagers were watching from a distance, the braver among them close enough to see clearly what was taking place. They ran quickly back to tell their less brave comrades. All the young men admired Shigar for his wit and courage. The mothers told their children that they must always remember Shigar's name.

Singing his praises they gathered together to thank him. "It is the will of God that everyone on earth should live in peace," said Shigar, once more back on his horse. "And His will should not be violated. Now that the dragon is dead, no other creature must live by bullying others. May you live in peace and happiness, and may your flocks and herds increase again."

The people went dancing after him to express their thanks and even after he had gone out of sight they gazed in the direction he had gone.

After this exploit Shigar returned to the island in the East Sea to see his first wife. She had not seen him for so long that she began to weep as soon as she caught sight of him. But her tears dried up when he told her all that he had done.

But then she did such a stupid thing! To prevent him from travelling far away again, she secretly cut through one wing of his horse in the night.

Shigar got up very early the next morning to go and see his second wife. He mounted his flying horse, which had the utmost difficulty in getting there and had to expend almost all its energy. The second wife also wept, but was also happy again when he told her how he had killed the python and the dragon.

But to keep him from travelling again, she secretly cut through the other wing of the horse in the night.

Shigar meant to go on another journey. One moonless night in June he got up even earlier than usual, silently led his horse out and mounted it. Without either wing the horse could only paw the air and turn round and round, neighing woefully. . . .

His wife hurried out. But Shigar and his horse fell into the sea before she could say a word.

"Shigar has fallen into the sea! Shigar has fallen into the sea!" The news reached the ears of the people and the birds and animals. No language could ever describe their sorrow. People came down in crowds to the seashore to mourn over him. The birds cawed and cried, asking the sea to give them back their hero. But only the crash and swell of the waves answered them. The birds were finally exhausted and flew away downcast. Yet they have not given up hope. Every year in June, there are

no birds to be seen on the plateau. They have all flown over the sea to ask for their Hero Shigar back.

The sea roars constantly, yet gives no answer.

Translated by Yu Fan-chin
Illustrations by Po Yi

The Third Son and the Magistrate

(A Story of the Chuang People)

Once upon a time, there was a very poor old man who kept his family by fashioning bamboo into all sorts of useful articles.

This old man had three sons. On his deathbed he told them: "Everyone should learn a trade. I've lived my life to bring you up. Now you'll have to earn your own living."

After the old man had said this, he breathed his last. With the little money he left them, the three sons bought a coffin and gave him the usual day's funeral service.

After the funeral they had only three coins left. So each of the three sons got one.

The eldest son was an idler. He did nothing but fool around all day. His coin was spent soon after the old man's death, and he died of hunger in the end because he was too lazy to do any work.

The second son was industrious. He learned to grow vegetables, bought seeds with the coin and became a good market gardener. Even so, he could barely make ends meet despite his industry.

The third son was still very young but he was thinking all the time what he could do to earn a living.

One day he saw some fishermen by the riverside. He watched them with great interest till he had learned their trade. Then he took the coin his father had left him, bought two fish-hooks and went to fish in the river every day. He caught a great many fish which he sold. In this way, he earned enough to feed himself and to have some money left to buy the things he needed. Soon he was quite a good fisherman.

But one day, he caught not even one fish although he had been sitting by the riverside for a long time. He was worrying over his bad luck, especially when he looked into the water and saw a huge fish, its eyes bulging, swishing its tail, swallowing in big gulps all the fish that he might have hooked. The third son got so angry that he grabbed his harpoon and threw it at the fish. With a splash, the speared fish turned over and sank to the bottom, the air slowly coming up in bubbles. Then the third son pulled the fish up on the bank by the rope fastened to the harpoon.

That day, he caught nothing but the one huge fish. So he decided to cook it for himself. When he cut its stomach open, he saw many small fish in it, a very beautiful golden carp among them. It was still alive, since its gills were opening and closing. The third son took pity on the beautiful creature and put it in a little copper basin that he filled with clear water. Soon the golden carp began moving around swishing its tail. As he looked at it admiringly, the third son liked it more and more. So he kept it and fed it with earthworms, duckweed and algae.

The golden carp grew more beautiful every day. The third son was so fond of it that he took it wherever he went, whether it was fishing, to market or to watch a play.

But one day, when he went to sell his fish, the third son did not take his carp along. When he came back, it had disappeared! He stood and stared at the empty copper basin, his tears dropping into it. From that day on, he felt unhappy and very lonely.

One day, he was fishing under a banian tree by the river. The cool breeze was caressing him and the river flowed so slowly that he dozed off. But suddenly he woke up. . . . He rubbed his eyes as he saw a young man of his own age bending over him, patting him on the shoulder and calling to him affectionately: "Don't you know me, sworn brother?" The third son thought this was very strange since he had not sworn to be brothers with anybody. Who could it be calling him that? "So you don't know me, eh?" the stranger said again. "I'm your close friend, and you're my benefactor." The third son was more puzzled than ever and did not know how to answer. At last the stranger said: "I was the golden carp whom you saved and took such good care of."

Then the third son began to understand. The golden carp, he was told, was the son of the Dragon King, the ruler of the water creatures. The other day, he had taken the shape of a golden carp while out to enjoy himself and the huge fish had swallowed him. It was only thanks to the third son that he was saved.

"You preserved my life, you kept me and fed me. Neither my father nor I shall ever forget your kindness. I've now come to invite you for a visit," the Dragon King's son continued.

"I'm glad to go with you," the third son replied. "But how can I proceed under water?"

"Close your eyes and hold on to me by my clothes!" the son of the Dragon King advised him.

The third son followed these instructions and saw a wide road stretching before him. Soon they came to the dragon palace with its pillars of red crystal, walls of yellow crystal and tiles of green crystal. How beautiful the different colours of crystal made this palace!

The Dragon King received the third son with much cordiality and gave him the best room and the best food. The son took him for walks in the garden where he saw many strange flowers and fruit. There were lichee nuts without stones, sweet as honey, "dragon's eyes" the size of a teacup, and juicy peaches. There were evergreen plantains and many other beautiful things in the garden such as he had never seen on earth.

The third son had been living for more than a month in the Dragon King's palace when, one day, he said to the son: "I'm only too grateful for your kindness and hospitality, sworn brother! But since there's no one else to look after my place, I'd better get back."

"If you really have to," the Dragon King's son agreed. "But you must come and visit us often. And one more thing: when my father wants to give you a present, ask for a white chicken."

The following morning, the third son went to take his leave from the Dragon King. Very kindly the king pointed to several rooms filled with gold and silver and said: "Take whatever you like of the precious things here!" The third son looked over the glittering gold bars, the silver, pearls and jewels, but then he remembered what the son had told him, and so he said instead: "I'm alone at home with enough to eat and wear, Dragon King, but sometimes I feel lonely. If you don't mind, I'd like to have a white chicken to keep me company." The Dragon King pondered this for a while, fingering his white beard, but finally he let the third son have the fowl.

The third son thereafter kept the white chicken in a cage. Back at home, he still went every day to fish and sell his catch. But every day there were dishes and rice on the table steaming when he returned!

At first, he thought that perhaps the neighbours had cooked food for him. But when he went to thank them, they were surprised—not one of them had done any cooking! The third son became so curious that he stayed at home one day to find out. However, not a soul came to cook for him. The next day, he went out to fish as usual. And when he came back, again there was a meal ready on the table. He wondered and wondered who it could be that prepared the food, so he could go and express his thanks. The next day, he only pretended to go fishing and turned back half-way. Peeping in through a crack in the door, he saw a girl in a white blouse and a coloured skirt standing before the stove cooking! He couldn't hold back any longer and called out: "How can I thank you, fair maiden?" But when the girl heard him, she clapped her hands, and suddenly turned into the white chicken, hiding in the cage.

The third son could do nothing but wait for another day. Again he pretended to go fishing, then turned back half-way and peeped in. Soon he saw the white chicken turning into a beautiful girl. Quickly he pushed the door open. Unable to get back to the cage, the girl stood shyly before him.

"You're so kind-hearted, fair maiden, you cook for me every day. . . . Who are you and where do you come from?"

"You needn't thank me," was the maiden's reply. "It really is nothing what I'm doing for you. I'm the Dragon King's daughter, I've come to pay our thanks to you for having saved my brother."

After that, they became man and wife and people came from far and near to congratulate them and to hear of the wonder of the third son marrying the Dragon King's daughter.

One day a flunkey of the county magistrate came by and reported immediately to his superior that he had seen a beautiful girl who came from the Dragon King's palace. From then on, the young couple was in for a lot of trouble. Within a few days, the magistrate summoned the third son to appear before him.

"In all villages, big and small, under my control everything is done according to my orders," the bully said to the third son. "Now my orders are that you send your wife to me within three days, or else your head will be cut off!"

"You can have everything but my wife," the young husband replied steadfastly. The magistrate wrinkled up his face in a wicked smile: "I can have everything, did you say? All right, then. Since you are a fisherman, bring me within three days one hundred and twenty carps of the same size and same red colour, each weighing exactly twelve ounces."

The third son was very worried when he came home and told his wife what the magistrate wanted. But she comforted him: "Don't you worry. I'll cope!" Then and there she cut one hundred and twenty carps of the same size out of a sheet of red paper, put them into a jar, poured cold water into it, and lo! the one hundred and twenty paper fish immediately turned into lively carps, all of the same red colour and the same size. Swimming around in the jar, they looked so lovely that the third son couldn't help looking at them with his mouth wide open with astonished pleasure. Then he had to take them to the magistrate.

Unable to get the better of the third son in their first encounter, the official bully now wanted something else: "I was told that your wife can weave very well," he said very haughtily. "Ask her to weave a bolt of blue cloth as long as the road, but she must have it done within three days." "Why do you demand one thing after another?" the third son asked. "Didn't you say I could have everything I wanted?" Knowing that it was no use to reason with him, the third son went home angry. Again his wife comforted him: "Don't you worry. I know what to do!" Thereupon she turned into a white fish and swam to the crystal palace to bring back with her a magic gourd which could grant them every wish.

When he held the gourd in his hands, the third son felt very happy. The third day, they sent a bolt of blue cloth to the magistrate as he had desired.

"How long is this piece of cloth?" the latter demanded to know. "As long as the road," the third son answered. "How do you know it's as long as the road?" bawled the magistrate. "You can measure it, if you like." So the magistrate ordered the cloth to be measured at once. They were at it a day and a night, yet the measuring was still going on. So, with ill grace, the magistrate said: "All right, we'll reckon you gave me right measure. But tomorrow you must bring me a flock of red sheep!"

When he had received the red sheep, he asked for water buffaloes and the third son had to get them for him. This went on, the magistrate demanding things and the third son fulfilling his demands. The magistrate became annoyed with the third son: "How is it that a poor person like you can give me everything I ask for? You must possess something magic. Hand it over to me!"

How greedy this magistrate was, demanding one thing after another! If I give him the magic gourd, what can I do if he still demands other things from me, thought the third son. So he said aloud: "I gave you everything you asked for. Where would I get a magic thing?"

The magistrate pounded the table in his fury. "You take my orders! Just one more word from you, and I'll have you locked up!"

The third son was ready to burst with anger. As soon as he was outside the yamen, he could contain himself no longer and cursed loudly: "Monster! Monster!"

The flunkey who overheard him ran in to report to the magistrate, so the third son was pursued and seized and thrown into a dark dungeon. The next day he was taken before the magistrate again. The official shouted at him at once: "You called me monster. Do you know what monsters look like? Bring me one hundred and twenty monsters in three days or I shall have your head!" There was nothing else to be done but promise. The third son went home and asked the advice of his wife. "What does he want the monsters for?" the wife wondered. "All right, he shall have them, but not the magic gourd." She asked the gourd for one hundred and twenty big cages and for twelve hundred catties of charcoal. Then she put ten catties of charcoal in each of the one hundred and twenty cages, pasted coloured paper over the cage, and poured oil into it. As soon as the oil was poured into the cages, they became alive as monsters of different forms that called without cease: "Monster! Monster!"

The third son then took these monsters to the magistrate's yamen. Of course, they attracted great attention on the way. By the time he reached the yamen, there were more people still watching. The magistrate ordered his flunkeys to drive the people away and put the monsters in an enclosure. "They really are monsters!" he said. "But what do they eat?" The third son replied: "Nothing but oil. And all you have to do is feed them up just once. They'll never need to feed on it again, and yet they won't die. You only need to keep them locked up."

The magistrate had nothing more to say after that and let the third son go home.

Actually, the magistrate was quite pleased with the monsters and intended to present them to the emperor for their queerness. At night, he had the monsters fed with a great deal of oil and properly cared for.

The monsters had big stomachs indeed! In one meal, they devoured twelve hundred catties of oil till their stomachs were bulging. And all through the night they kept shrieking and screaming. Thinking that something might have happened to them, the magistrate at last lit a lantern and went out to have a look. As soon as he came near the monsters with his lantern, all of them caught fire, and ran around like mad. The whole yamen was on fire in an instant and burned down, and the magistrate, the other officials and all the flunkeys perished with it.

Translated by Yu Fan-chin
Illustration by Ju Min-kang

The Frog Who Became an Emperor

(A Story of the Chuang People)

Once upon a time there lived a very poor couple. A baby was on the way when the husband was forced to leave his home to find a living somewhere far away. Before he left, he embraced his wife fondly and looked long at her. Then he gave her the last few silver pieces he had, saying, "When the child is born, you must do all you can to bring it up. You and I are so poor that we are of no use. But our child may be able to help us find a living."

Three months after her husband's departure, the wife gave birth. The baby was neither a boy nor a little girl, but a frog!

The poor mother was heart-broken, and wept bitterly.

"Ah, an animal, not a child!" she cried. "Not only he, but even I, his mother, will be ashamed to meet anyone."

She thought at first she would do away with him, but she did not have the heart to do so. She wanted to bring him up, but was afraid of what the neighbours would say.

As she brooded over the matter, she remembered her husband's words before he went away, and she decided not to kill the child but always keep him hidden under the bed. In this way, no one knew she had given birth to a frog-child. But within two months, the frog-child had grown so big that he could no longer be kept under the bed. And one day, he suddenly spoke in a human voice.

"Mother," he said, "my father is coming back tonight. I am going to wait for him beside the road."

And sure enough, the husband did come home that very night.

"Have you seen your son?" the wife asked anxiously.

"Where? Where is my son?"

"He was waiting for you by the side of the road. Didn't you see him?"

"No! I saw no sign of anyone," her husband answered, surprised. "All I saw was an awful frog which gave me such a fright."

"That frog was your son," said the wife unhappily.

When the husband heard that his wife had given birth to a frog, he was grieved.

"Why did you tell him to meet me?" he said. "Wasn't that a strange thing to do?"

"What do you mean, tell him to meet you? He went without any telling from me. He suddenly said you were coming tonight and went out to meet you."

"This is really extraordinary," thought the husband, brightening up. "No one knew I was coming. How could he have known?"

"Call him home, quickly," he said aloud. "He might catch cold outside."

Just as the mother opened the door to do so, the frog came in. He hopped over to his father, who asked him, "Was it you I met on the road?"

"Yes," said the frog. "I was waiting for you, Father."

"How did you know I was coming back tonight?"

"I know everything under heaven."

The father and mother were amazed by his words and more amazed when he went on.

"Our country is in great peril," he said solemnly. "We are unable to resist the invaders. I want Father to take me to the emperor, for I must save our country."

"How can that be?" said the father. "Firstly, you have no horse. Secondly, you have no weapons, and thirdly, you have never been on a battlefield. How, then, do you propose to fight?"

The frog was very much in earnest. "Only take me there," he pleaded. "I'll defeat the enemy, never fear."

The father could not dissuade the frog, so he took his frog-son to the city to seek an audience with the emperor. After two days' journey, they arrived at the capital, where they saw the Imperial Decree displayed.

"The imperial capital is in danger. My country has been invaded. We are willing to marry our daughter to the man who can drive away the enemy. . . ."

The frog stretched out his hand, tore down the decree and with one gulp swallowed it. The soldier guarding the Imperial Decree was greatly alarmed. He could hardly imagine a frog accepting such a responsible duty. However, since the frog had swallowed the decree, he must be taken into the palace.

The emperor asked the frog if he had the means and ability to defeat the enemy. The frog replied, "Yes, Lord." Then the emperor asked him how many men and horses he would need.

"Not a single horse or a single man," answered the frog. "All I need is a heap of hot, glowing embers."

The emperor immediately commanded that a heap of hot, glowing embers be brought and it was done. Flickering flames from the embers leaped high into the air and the heat was intense. The frog sat before the fire devouring the flames by the mouthful for three days and three nights. He ate till his belly was as big and round as a bladder full of fat. By now the city was in great danger, for the enemy was already at the walls. The emperor was terribly apprehensive, but the frog behaved as if nothing unusual was happening, and calmly went on swallowing fire and flame. Only after the third day had passed did he go to the top of the city wall and look at the situation. There, ringing the city, were thousands of soldiers and horses in serried ranks, as far as the eye could see.

"How, frog, are you going to drive back the enemy?" asked the emperor.

"Order your troops to stop plying their bows," replied the frog. "And open the city gate."

The emperor turned pale with alarm when he heard these words.

"What! With the enemy at our very door! You tell me to open the gate! How dare you trifle with me?"

"Your Imperial Highness has bidden me drive the enemy away," said the frog. "And that being so, you must heed my words."

The emperor was helpless. He ordered the soldiers to stop bending their bows and lay down their arrows and throw open the gate.

poured in. The frog was above them in the gate-tower and, as they passed underneath, he coolly and calmly spat fire down on them, searing countless men and horses. They fled back in disorder.

The emperor was overjoyed when he saw that the enemy was defeated. He made the frog a general and ordered that the victory should be celebrated for several days. But of the princess he said nothing. To tell the truth, he had not the slightest intention of letting his daughter marry a frog.

"Of course I cannot do such a thing!" he said to himself. Instead, he let it be known that it was the princess who refused. She must marry someone else, but whom? He did not know what to do. Anyone but a frog! Finally he ordained that her marriage should be decided by casting the Embroidered Ball.

Casting the Embroidered Ball! The news spread immediately throughout the whole country and within a few days the city was in a turmoil. Men from far and wide came to try their luck, and all manner of people flocked to the capital. The day came. The frog was present. He did not push his way into the mob but stood at the very edge of the crowded square.

A gaily festooned pavilion of a great height had been built. The emperor led the princess and her train of maids, dressed in scarlet and green, to their seats high up on the stand.

The moment arrived. The princess tossed the Embroidered Ball into the air, and down it gently floated. The masses in the square surged and roared like a raging sea. As one and all stretched eager hands to clutch the ball, the frog drew in a mighty breath and, like a whirling tornado, sucked the ball straight to him.

Now, surely, the princess will have to marry the frog! But the emperor was still unwilling to let this happen.

"An Embroidered Ball cast by a princess," he declared, "can only be seized by a human hand. No beast may do so."

He told the princess to throw down a second ball.

This time a young, stalwart fellow caught the ball.

"This is the man!" cried the happy emperor. "Here is the person fit to be my imperial son-in-law."

A sumptuous feast was set to celebrate the occasion.

Can you guess who that young stalwart fellow was? Of course it was the frog, now in the guise of a man.

Not till he was married to the princess did he change back again. By day he was a frog but at night he stripped off his green skin and was transformed into a fine, upstanding youth.

The princess could not keep it a secret and one day revealed it to her father, the emperor. He was startled but happy.

"At night," he said to his son-in-law, "you discard your outer garment, I hear, and become a handsome young man. Why do you wear that horrid frog-skin in the day?"

"Ah, Sire," replied the frog, "this outer garment is priceless. When I wear it in winter, I am warm and cosy; and in summer, cool and fresh. It is proof against wind and rain. Not even the fiercest flame can set it alight. And as long as I wear it, I can live for thousands of years."

"Let me try it on!" demanded the emperor.

"Yes, Sire," replied the frog and made haste to discard his skin.

The emperor smiled gleefully. He took off his dragon-embroidered robe and put on the frog-skin. But then he could not take it off again!

The frog put on the imperial robe and became the emperor. His father-in-law remained a frog for ever.

Olive Lake

(A Story of the Han People)

Long, long ago, a mother and her son lived by Olive Lake below Olive Mountain. The mother was very, very old and could not work any more. Her young son rented a plot of land from the landlord and laboured on it all the year round. But despite his industry year in and year out, their life never improved; they never had enough food or clothing.

The young man began to marvel: "Why is it that the water in Olive Lake, that doesn't stay still, is yet turbid? Why is it that, in spite of all my hard work, I still am so poor?"

Then he heard that one could seek advice from the God of the West in one's difficulties and decided to go there and find an answer to his questions.

He was not one to let a matter rest, once he had decided on it. So he made sure that the stocks of fuel, rice, oil and salt would last his mother for some time. Then he set off the very next morning.

For seven times seven days he walked, his face turned towards the west. Parched with thirst, he knocked at a hut and asked for a drink.

The kind old woman inside invited him into her house and treated him hospitably. Then she asked him: "Why is it, young man, that you're panting so? Where are you hurrying to?"

"I am going to the Western Heaven," he replied, "to ask the God of the West why the water of Olive Lake, although it never stays still, is yet turbid and why I labour all the year round and am still poor."

When the old woman heard this, she gladly seized the opportunity. "Will you find out something for me too? I have a daughter, eighteen years of age, who is very beautiful and clever. Yet she has never spoken a word in all her life! Would you ask the God of the West why she cannot speak?"

"I shall ask for you," the young man promised readily.

After a night in the old woman's hut, he walked on towards the west again, for another seven times seven days. At the end of that period, he felt very tired. As it was getting dark, he knocked at the door of a hut.

An old man opened and invited him in. After he had put some food and drink before him, he inquired: "Where are you going in such a hurry that you're sweating all over?"

"I am going to the Western Heaven to ask the God of the West why the water in Olive Lake doesn't stay still and yet is turbid, and why is it that I labour all the year and am still poor," the young man answered.

Thereupon the old man said with a laugh: "How very fortunate! I too have a question. There's an orange tree in my orchard, with leaves a lush green. But why doesn't it bear fruit?"

"I shall be glad to find out for you," the young man promised readily. The next day, he continued his journey.

Suddenly he came to a wide, wild river. There was no ferry. How could he get across? He sat down on a big stone by the riverside, wondering what to do. Suddenly, a gust of wind covered the sky with dark clouds and sent the river roaring. After a while, the storm subsided and a beautifully coloured cloud appeared in the sky. From the rushing river, a dragon called up:

"Hey, young man! Where is it that you're travelling to with such speed?"

"I am going to the Western Heaven to ask the God of the West why the water in Olive Lake doesn't stay still and yet is turbid, and why is it that I labour all the year and yet am so poor," the young man replied.

"Then you can ask a question for me, too. I harm neither men nor animals, and I've chastised myself for a thousand years here. Why can't I rise up to Heaven?"

"I'll be sure to ask this question for you," the young man promised the dragon readily, and then the dragon carried him across the river on his back. After the young man had gone westward for more than a day, he came to a big, old city with a palace. When he asked the gateman where the God of the West lived, he was taken to a magnificent hall in the palace. In the middle of this hall sat an old man with silvery hair and beard. This must be the God of the West, thought the young man. But before he could utter a word, the old man addressed him smilingly:

"What is it you come here for, young man?"

"I have four questions to which I would like you to give me the answers."

The God of the West assented, but first told him: "Our rule here is: ask one and not two; ask three and not four; ask only odd but no even numbers of questions. Now you have four questions. Think it over and decide which one to omit!"

The young man was hard put to it to decide. He thought the questions over and over again. His own question was very important. But the three other questions were also important. Perhaps he'd better put other people's business before his own, since he was allowed to ask only three questions and not four. So he decided to give up his own question and ask the three others.

When they were answered satisfactorily, he went away happily from the palace of the God of the West.

At the riverside, the dragon was waiting for him: "What about my question?"

"The God of the West said you must do two good deeds before you can rise up to Heaven."

"What deeds? Tell me quickly!" the dragon urged him.

"Carrying me across the river is one. The other good deed will be to knock off the pearl which shines on your head at night."

Again the dragon carried the young man across the river and then asked him to help knock the pearl off. Two horns shot out from the dragon's head and he rose up towards Heaven immediately. When he was piercing the clouds, he called down to the young man:

"Take the pearl as my reward for you!"

The young man took the shining pearl and went on his homeward journey. When he arrived at the old man's place, the first question asked was: "Did you do as you promised?"

"Yes, I did. And the God of the West wants me to tell you that nine jars of gold and nine jars of silver are buried at the bottom of the pool in your orchard. If you dig the jars out and water the orange tree with the water from the pool, the tree will bear fruit."

The old man called his son and together they scooped the water out of the pool. Then they started to dig, the young man helping them. They dug for some time, but neither gold nor silver appeared. But they did not give up. They dug deeper and deeper and there—they found nine jars of gold and nine jars of silver! As soon as they had taken the jars out, clear water sprang from the bottom of the pool and filled it in a moment.

The old man watered the tree with the clear water, as he had been advised. And as soon as the water was sprinkled on it, every branch of the tree bore fruit. Soon the whole tree was laden with golden oranges. The old man was so happy that he didn't know what to say.

The young man was asked to stay for a couple of days more and rewarded with a lot of the gold and silver. Then the young man took his leave and went on till he arrived at the old woman's house, carrying with him the pearl that shone at night and the gold and the silver.

The old woman ran out to meet him and inquired: "Have you done what I asked you to do?"

"Yes," he answered. "The God of the West wants me to tell you that your daughter will be able to speak when she sees a young man after her own heart."

The girl came in while her mother was talking to the young man. She blushed like a rose when she caught sight of the young man and smiled shyly. Then she asked slowly: "Who is this, Mother?"

The old woman was so happy that she reeled in her excitement, clasping the girl in her arms and shedding tears of joy. Since the young man was so brawny and honest, she advised her daughter:

"This is a day of good omen, my child, since you spoke your first words today. Let it be the day of your marriage!"

The young man then took leave from the old woman and went happily towards home, with his pearl that shone at night, his gold and silver, and his young bride.

When he reached home, he found that his aged mother had cried her eyes blind with longing for her son.

The young man wanted his mother to see how clever and beautiful her daughter-in-law was, but all she could do was to feel the girl's smooth cheeks. He also wanted her to see the gold and silver. But she could only listen to the clinking of the metal. Then he took out the pearl and waved it before her eyes. But no matter how the pearl shone, all the mother saw was darkness.

The young man felt very unhappy. He thought fervently: "If only my mother could see!" At the very thought, his mother's eyes became seeing again.

The young man was amazed that his wish was instantly fulfilled. Waving the pearl, he thought again: "If there were no wealthy men in the village, the poor would not be oppressed!" And it did happen that all the wealthy men died.

The young man then understood that the pearl was not an ordinary pearl, that it could not only shine at night, but grant people's wishes.

From that day on, the water in Olive Lake was no more turbid and the life of the poor became sweet as honey.

Translated by Yu Fan-chin

How the Brothers Divided Their Property

(A Story of the Tung People)

Long, long ago, there were two brothers living in a village. The older one was called Big Lang, the younger Little Lang. Their parents had died very early, leaving them nothing but a small plot of poor land, an ox and a yellow dog.

Big Lang was a lazy fellow. Instead of going to the fields, he stayed at home all day, leaving the work of taking care of the ox and ploughing the land entirely to his younger brother.

One day, Big Lang had a brilliant idea. "Grown trees have more branches; grown-up children divide their property. Both of us are grown up now," he said to his younger brother. "So let's divide our property and live separately."

"We're doing well together," Little Lang answered. "Why should we separate?"

But Big Lang got angry at him. "We have to separate, I tell you! You always wait till I do the cooking for you. I won't do it any more!"

Since Little Lang was unable to persuade him otherwise, the two brothers separated. Big Lang kept the ox and the better part of the land, giving Little Lang the worse part and the dog.

After they had divided the property, Big Lang continued to be as lazy as ever. The ox grew thinner and thinner with hunger till it could only stagger, since Big Lang didn't take the trouble to look after it properly. Little Lang's dog, however, was well fed. Every day, Little Lang took the animal with him to the mountains while he chopped wood, and so both lived quite a good, healthy life.

When the time came for the spring ploughing, Little Lang was very worried because he did not have an ox, so much so that he could hardly eat anything.

One day, while he was dozing fretfully before the fire, the dog barked at him. Little Lang woke up with a start, quickly shouldered his hoe and sickle, and went to the fields. After working for some time, he became tired and sat down on the ground panting. Again the dog barked at him. "Yellow dog, yellow dog, what are you barking for? Can you do the ploughing for me?"

The dog walked back and forth in the field, as if he were pulling a plough. Thereupon Little Lang decided that he should use the dog as a draught animal. He fashioned a plough small enough for the dog to pull, and thus he ploughed every day.

Big Lang was surprised when he saw how well-ploughed Little Lang's land was. He wanted to know how it had been done.

"Who ploughed for you, Little Lang?" he asked.

"I did it myself."

"Where did you get an ox?"

"Don't I have my yellow dog?"

Big Lang was even more surprised when he heard that a dog could plough. So he borrowed Little Lang's dog to try it.

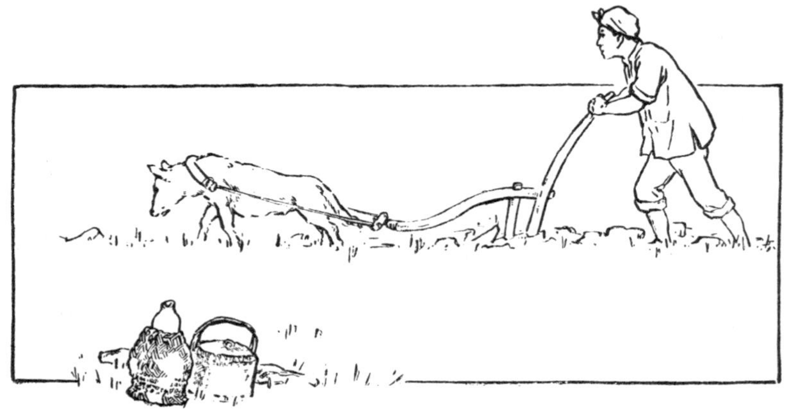

But the dog wouldn't move a single step on Big Lang's field. Finally he got so angry that he whipped the poor animal to death.

It was getting dark and the dog hadn't returned, so Little Lang went to his brother's to inquire.

"Brother, where is my dog?"

"God knows where your beast has died!"

Big Lang's dark face stopped Little Lang from asking any more. He went to look everywhere but did not see a sign of his dog. At last he found him, lying quite stiff beside a fence. Grief-stricken, Little Lang picked up his dog and carried it home, crying out on the way:

I got a dog when our possessions we divided.
It helped me plough, and never did I chide it!
Now someone's killed my dog—how can I abide it?
Deep is my grief, I cannot hide it!

Little Lang buried the dog under a mound and visited the grave every morning.

One day, he found a shiny golden bamboo shoot growing out of the mound. When he went there again that night, it had grown into a beautiful, tall bamboo tree. Little Lang was so happy that he shook the bamboo by one of its branches and sang:

Money tree, my treasure cask,
Drop some gold now! Silver coins at dusk!

Thousand ounces gold at sunrise let me ask,
Thousand catties silver be your evening task!

As soon as he had finished singing, gold, silver and pearls began raining down on him. He quickly filled his pockets with these riches. From then on, he sang and shook the bamboo every time he visited the dog's grave, and every time gold and silver fell to the ground.

"Little Lang, where have you stolen all this?" Big Lang asked him when he saw his brother in possession of so much gold and silver.

"I didn't steal anything. I shook it down from the bamboo on the dog's grave."

"Are you telling the truth? And is there any more?" Big Lang asked again.

"Of course there is! All you need to do is shake the bamboo and down the gold and silver will drop."

"How do you shake the bamboo?"

Little Lang very honestly told his brother how it was done.

Immediately Big Lang took two baskets and ran off to the grave mound. He gripped the bamboo that had grown out of the grave of the yellow dog and was just going to sing, when caterpillars dropped on his head, his face and his hands till he was covered with them. Not only that—they crawled inside his clothes till he rolled on the ground, mad with the itching pain they caused.

As soon as he could, Big Lang got up and ran home for a big knife with which he chopped down the bamboo tree in his rage.

The next day, Little Lang went to visit the dog's grave as usual. How sad he was to find the bamboo chopped down! Carrying it home, he cried all the way:

I got a dog when our possessions we divided.
It helped me plough, and never did I chide it!
Now someone's killed my dog—how can I abide it?
Deep is my grief, I cannot hide it!
On my dog's grave a bamboo grew,
Gave gold in the morning, silver in the evening dew.
Who's cut down my dear bamboo
And caused poor me to grieve anew?

Little Lang split the bamboo and made a big coop for chickens from it. This he put outside in a corner, intending to sell it at the next fair. But it happened that many hens from the neighbourhood and even hen pheasants came and laid their eggs in the coop So Little Lang got a lot of eggs in one day.

He was happy again, as he went out to sell the eggs.

"Where have you stolen the eggs, Little Lang?" his brother came to ask when he heard about it.

"I didn't steal them! The fowls and hen pheasants laid them in the coop I'd made."

"Lend me your coop for a month then, Little Lang!"

Good-natured as he was, Little Lang lent the coop to his older brother.

Big Lang put the coop under the eaves of his house. Soon fowls and hen pheasants came cackling and crowded into the coop one after another.

Big Lang quickly went to see. But when he put his hand into the coop, he didn't find any eggs, only birds' droppings. He got so angry that he stamped on the coop till it was nothing but splinters and then set it afire.

Little Lang was greatly saddened to find that his brother had burned the coop. He collected the ashes and carried them home, crying all the way:

I got a dog when our possessions we divided.
It helped me plough, and never did I chide it!
Now someone's killed my dog—how can I abide it?
Deep is my grief, I cannot hide it!
On my dog's grave a bamboo grew,
Gave gold in the morning, silver in the evening dew.
Who's cut down my dear bamboo
And caused poor me to grieve anew?
A bamboo coop with it I made
Where eggs the fowls and pheasants laid.

Who burned my coop? Who made this raid
And left me sad and sore dismayed?

Little Lang had nothing left—his dog, the bamboo tree that gave him gold and silver, the coop in which birds had laid their eggs, all were gone. So he went out all alone to clear a piece of land in the mountains with his hoe. This he sowed with pumpkin seeds after he had fertilized it with ashes from the coop.

The seeds came up very fast. There were sprouts on the first day and leaves on the second. The vines appeared on the third and covered the slope on the fourth. On the fifth the whole mountain was covered with golden pumpkin blossoms, and on the sixth day the vines were heavy with ripe pumpkins! The biggest one stood eight or nine feet round so that two men couldn't have circled it with arms outstretched. It looked so remarkable that Little Lang called it the "King of the Pumpkins."

A monkey passing by saw the pumpkins there and picked one. Then he hurried with the news to the other monkeys in their cave: "There are a lot of pumpkins on a mountain-side, go and pick some quickly!"

At night the monkeys came in droves and took away half the pumpkins. Little Lang was very annoyed next day when he discovered that so many of his pumpkins had been stolen.

That night, he went to watch over his pumpkins. He bored a hole into the "King of the Pumpkins" and hid there to find out who the thief was.

At midnight, the monkeys came again and took the remaining pumpkins away except the "King of the Pumpkins" which was too heavy for them.

Because they couldn't carry the "King" away, they decided to ask their guardian fairy's help. Thereupon, the small monkeys quickly ran back to their cave and fetched their gold and silver cups. These they placed in front of the "King of the Pumpkins," then lit red candles and incense sticks, and kowtowed in supplication, for their guardian fairy to descend.

Hidden inside the pumpkin, Little Lang saw and heard everything. Suddenly he gave a shout: "Tai!" Thinking it was the "King of the Pumpkins" shouting, the monkeys were frightened and scattered, leaving their gold and silver cups behind.

When the hubbub had quieted down on the outside, Little Lang crept slowly out of the pumpkin and went home with the gold and silver cups.

Again Big Lang came to inquire how he had obtained them.

"Where did you steal these cups, Little Lang?"

"They aren't stolen! I picked them up in the pumpkin field last night."

And he told Big Lang how he had fertilized the pumpkins with the ashes from the coop, how one pumpkin had grown to a tremendous size and how the monkeys had been stealing the pumpkins.

When it was all dark, Big Lang went to his brother's field and crept inside the "King of Pumpkins," as Little Lang had done. The monkeys came again, more and more of them, but without cups this time. All together they picked up the huge pumpkin. The jogging movement they made with the giant pumpkin sent Big Lang to sleep after a very short journey.

The monkeys dragged the "King of the Pumpkins" across gullies and ridges. Big Lang woke up when they reached the edge of a sheer precipice. When he heard the noise the monkeys made, he thought they were appealing to their guardian fairy to descend. So he shouted "Hey!" Hearing the "King of the Pumpkins" shout again, as they thought, the monkeys threw it down and ran for their lives. The "King of the Pumpkins" tumbled down the mountain, faster and faster, till it reached the bottom, smashed to smithereens. And Big Lang, inside it, was smashed up, too.

Translated by Yu Fan-chin
Illustration by Ju Min-kang

Stories About Nasrdin Avanti

(From the Uighur People)

I'm Wrong

One night, Avanti was passing by a graveyard. Some horsemen galloping in the same direction made him suspicious that they might not be up to anything good. So he lowered himself into a freshly dug grave and hid there. But the horsemen had seen him slip down and were wondering in turn what he was up to. So they came up and shouted at him: "Who are you?"

Avanti put his head out of the grave and answered them:

"Oh, I'm one of the dead men buried in this graveyard."

"And what does a dead man want to be up for at this time of night?"

"Just to get some fresh air."

"Does a dead man need fresh air too?"

"Ah yes, yes. . . . You're right, and I'm wrong!"

So saying, Avanti crept back into the grave again.

Hiding from the Thief

One day a thief broke into Avanti's house. Avanti saw him and hid in a chest.

The thief ransacked the house without finding anything worth taking. In the end he opened the chest and saw Avanti. "Aha!" he said, "and what are you doing inside the chest?"

"I was ashamed that there was nothing in my house that would appeal to your taste. That's why I hid here," Avanti confessed.

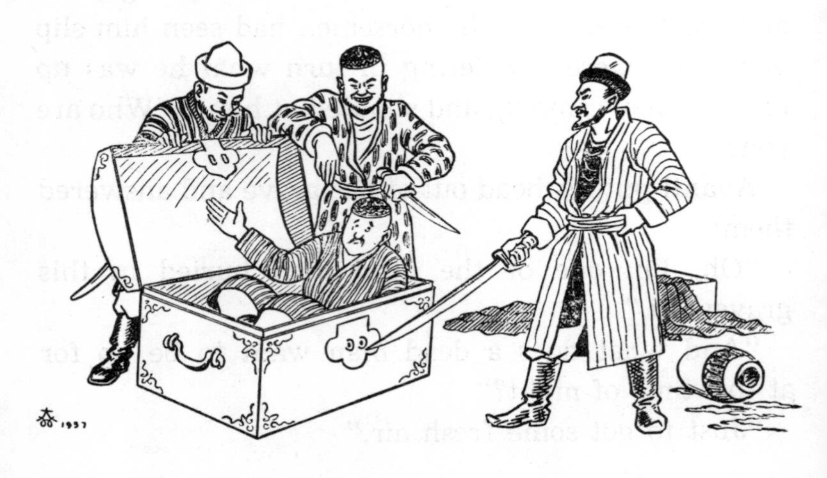

Avanti Moves House

One night several thieves broke into Avanti's home. Hurriedly they packed up his furniture and belongings and made off.

They were barely half-way across the yard when Avanti followed close at their heels carrying some small articles in his hands.

"Hello Avanti, where are you going so late at night?" one of the thieves saw him and queried.

"Well," said Avanti, "I've been wanting to move for a long time but I couldn't afford a cart for my things. It's very kind of you to help me."

A Bargain Made Even

One day Avanti went to the market to buy himself a pair of trousers. Having settled the bargain, he was just about to pay for them when he changed his mind. "After all, this pair of trousers I'm wearing isn't quite finished yet," he muttered to himself. Then he turned to the shopkeeper and said: "Better exchange these for a shirt, please!"

The shopkeeper saw nothing wrong in this request and handed him a shirt. Avanti snatched it from the man and walked off without paying for it. The shopkeeper sprang to his feet shouting: "Why aren't you paying for what you bought?"

"Haven't I given you the trousers whose price we had already settled?" retorted Avanti.

Selling a Cow

Avanti's wife wanted to sell their cow, which was bad-tempered and barren, so Avanti took the animal to market.

Customers came and looked at the cow, but all walked away without buying her, because Avanti kept saying: "You may not be able to get any milk from this cow, but she's quite capable of horning you!" Why should anybody have wanted to buy the cow after such a recommendation?

A cattle-dealer who had listened for a while was greatly amused by Avanti's naivety and said to him: "You'd better let me sell this cow for you."

"You are very kind," Avanti said. "May you prosper! Take charge of her then." With this, Avanti handed him the rope by which he held the cow.

As soon as the cattle-dealer had taken over, he began his spiel.

"Look at this cow — how gentle she is! And not only that — she'll give you fifteen bowls of milk every day. You won't be sorry to have bought her!"

At that, Avanti took the cow's rope out of the cattle-dealer's hand again and said: "If she is gentler than a lamb and gives fifteen bowls of milk every day, why should I sell her?"

Ask the Cow Herself

Having bought a cow in the market, Avanti made his way home. "What a nice cow, Avanti!" said the passers-by. "How much did she cost you?" He was getting very annoyed by having to repeat the same answer over and over again. Finally, when another two men asked him the same question, he pointed at the cow and said: "Kind gentlemen, why should you all bother me so? If you want to know, why don't you ask the cow herself?"

Jump into the Water!

One day in winter Avanti set out for a journey, taking his donkey loaded with firewood along. He was freezing, and thinking of the donkey he said to himself: "The donkey must be freezing too in this weather. I'd better light the firewood on his back, then he'll get warmed up." No sooner said than done. The dry wood flared up at once. Frightened, the donkey galloped away as fast as his legs could carry him. Avanti ran after the animal, shouting: "If you're smart enough, jump into the water!"

His Tail Is in the Bag

Avanti was going to market with a donkey for sale. On the way, the donkey's tail got so dirty that Avanti thought to himself: "Quite possibly his dirty tail will displease the customers. That won't do!" So he cut off the donkey's tail and kept it in his saddle-bag.

At the market, a man came and cast a glance at the donkey. "A nice donkey," he said, "but what a pity he has no tail!"

"If you've taken a fancy to this donkey," Avanti said, "tell me how much you'd like to pay for him. His tail is in the bag here!"

The Moon

Someone asked Avanti: "What becomes of the old moon every time a new moon comes up?"

Avanti replied: "When the crescent moon comes up, Allah cuts the old moon into little pieces and makes stars of them."

The Sun or the Moon?

Nasrdin Avanti was asked by a friend: "Which is better, the moon or the sun?"

"The moon, of course," said Avanti.

"Why do you think so?" asked the friend.

"Look," replied Avanti, "the sun comes out during the daytime, but it really makes no difference, anyway, since it's always bright then. However if it were not for the moon, it would be pitch dark all round at night."

Fish Will Climb a Tree

Avanti was asked: "If water is set on fire, what'll happen to all the fish in it?"

"They'll climb up a tree, of course!"

In All Directions

One day Avanti's friends asked him: "Why do people go hither and thither in all directions as soon as it dawns?"

"Aiya, isn't it a pity to see how foolish you are!" was Avanti's rejoinder. "Isn't it quite clear? If all the people go in the same direction, won't the earth list on that side and turn over?"

Write for Me

One of Avanti's friends came to him saying: "I have a brother living in the capital. Would you mind writing him a letter for me?"

"But I don't think I have time to go to the city!" said Avanti.

"I'm not asking you to go to the city," the friend explained. "I only asked if you wouldn't be kind enough to write him a letter."

"I understood you perfectly the first time," Avanti replied. "But nobody can decipher my handwriting except myself. So if I'm not there to read it to him, it's no use writing. That's why I say I am not going to the capital."

It's No Good to Be Inside

Someone asked Avanti: "When you attend a funeral, is it better to walk ahead of the coffin or behind it?"

Avanti looked hard at the questioner before he answered: "Either will do, as long as you aren't inside it!"

The Only Remedy

A neighbour intended to make fun of Avanti and told him: "Last night, a mouse crept into my stomach while I was sleeping. What shall I do?"

"What you must do at once is to find yourself a live cat and swallow it. That's the only remedy for you," was Avanti's immediate rejoinder.

Expiation

Once, Avanti found a stray sheep. He took it home, killed it and ate it. A friend heard of this and asked him:

"What will you say to our Lord about this sin when you're called before Him on Judgement Day?"

"I shall say that I haven't eaten the sheep."

"But that won't do. What if the sheep appears to give witness?"

"If the sheep appears? That'll be just fine! I'll take it back to its owner and settle the whole business."

At the Barber's

Avanti went to a barber's to have his head shaved.

The inexperienced barber cut him in several places which he dressed with cotton-wool. Standing up after the ordeal and looking at himself in the mirror, Avanti exclaimed:

"What a gifted pair of hands you have! Now that you've planted cotton on one half of my head, I can go home and plant linseed on the other." So saying, he went away.

Wife and Pancake

Avanti and his wife sat on the floor chatting. Feeling hungry, Avanti asked her: "Don't you have any pancakes around?"

"Can't you be satisfied with sitting here and looking at your beautiful wife?"

"Of course, I can," said Avanti. "But if I could have a pancake to eat while looking at your beautiful face, that would be even better!"

Path Along the Tree-tops

One day a bunch of naughty children wanted to make fun of Avanti and said to him: "There are birds' eggs on that tree, Avanti. Won't you get them for us, please? We can't climb up."

Not to disappoint the children, Avanti was ready to climb the tree. But knowing that the mischievous youngsters would make off with his boots if he left them on the ground, he tied them to his waist-band before he started the climb.

"We'll take care of your boots for you, Avanti!" the children said.

"No, thank you!" was the reply. "I'm a busy man. And as soon as I've got the eggs for you, I'll make my way home along the tree-tops."

Baggage of Two Asses

King Tomur and his favourite courtier went hunting and took Avanti along. On the way, when Tomur and the courtier began to feel hot, they took off their coats and let Avanti carry them on his back. When Tomur saw that Avanti was sweating like anything, he mocked at him.

"Avanti, you're carrying as much baggage as an ass!"

But Avanti was quick with the retort: "No, my lord, I'm carrying the baggage of two asses."

The Thirsty Pouch

One day Avanti attended a wedding. One of the guests not only ate a lot of the sweetmeats of-

fered, but stuffed his pouch with them. When Avanti saw what he was doing, he picked up a tea pot and quietly, from behind, poured some tea into the guest's pouch. When the guest discovered what Avanti had done, he was not at all abashed but reproached Avanti.

"What's my pouch got to do with you that you come and pour tea into it?"

"I meant no harm," was Avanti's defence. "When I saw how many sweets your pouch had tucked away, I was afraid it would get thirsty. That's why I gave it a drink."

What Does the Owl Say?

Avanti bragged about himself saying: "I understand the language of the birds."

The king heard about this and took him along on a hunt. On their way they saw a wall in ruins and an owl hooting above it. So the king asked Avanti: "What does the owl say?"

"Well," Avanti answered, "it says that if the king keeps on riding roughshod over the people, his kingdom will soon crumble just like its nest did."

The Ring

One of Avanti's friends, a business man, came to say goodbye to him before setting out for a long journey. He saw Avanti wearing a golden ring and schemed to get it.

"Avanti," said the friend. "I can't live in peace if I don't see you for a long time. I'll be missing you so much when I am away! Why don't you let me have your ring for the sake of our friendship? Whenever I look at it, I'll then feel like seeing you in the flesh and this'll be a great comfort to me."

But the ring was the only valuable thing Avanti had ever had in his life and he would not give it away.

So he replied: "I'm deeply grateful for your kind sentiments. But I too cannot live in peace, if I have to miss you for a long time. Be merciful and let me keep the ring! Whenever I look at it, I'll remember how my friend asked me for it, but I didn't give it to him, and so it'll constantly remind me of you."

The Guest and Honey

Once Avanti was a guest at a friend's place and was treated to cheese, pancakes and honey. Avanti stuffed himself with all the pancakes and the cheese. Then he started on the honey, although there were no pancakes left to eat with it. At that, his host admonished him: "You can't eat honey without pancakes! It'll upset you!"

Having swallowed the last drop of honey, Avanti merely said:

"Only God knows who will be upset in the end. May He pour His blessings over you. . . . " And without another word, he was off.

Good Advice

One day Avanti thought of earning some money. So he took a length of rope, about twenty or thirty feet, and went to the market-place. Just as he got there and stopped among a group of porters, a man came up and said:

"I've a crate full of bowls and cups here. Whoever carries it home for me shall get three pieces of good advice as his pay."

Hearing this, all the porters ignored him. Avanti, however, bethought himself: "A thing like money can be obtained at any time, but good advice is difficult to get. I'd better hear what advice he has to give, in order to learn something." So he agreed to carry the crate for the man.

As they were walking along, Avanti said to the owner of the crate: "How about telling me now what good advice you have to give?"

The owner of the crate said: "Don't believe anybody who tells you that it is better to go hungry than to eat your fill."

"That's very good advice!" Avanti agreed.

They walked on for a little while, then Avanti said: "Well, let's have the second piece of advice now."

"Don't believe anybody who tells you that it is better to go on foot than to ride on horseback."

"Aiya! That really is excellent advice!" Avanti exclaimed.

After they had gone on for some distance, Avanti demanded to hear the third piece of advice.

"Don't believe anyone who tells you that there are porters even more foolish than you," the man said. But hardly had he finished when Avanti suddenly let go of the rope in his hand and said:

"And don't you believe anyone, either, who tells you that the bowls and cups in this crate aren't broken!"

Difficult Questions

Three tradesmen once came to a certain kingdom and were entertained by the king in his palace. After a few days' stay, they said that each of them had a difficult question to ask of the king. The king listened with great attention to their questions, but not one of them could he answer. He summoned his counsellors, orators and magicians, but they were of no help either.

Ashamed and annoyed, the king grumbled: "Isn't there a single wise man in my kingdom to answer the questions of our guests?"

Thereupon one man stood up and said: "There is no one who can answer their questions except Avanti. If it pleases Your Majesty, I suggest that he be summoned."

The king immediately issued a summons for Avanti. Stick in hand, Avanti rode straight up to the king on his donkey and dismounted.

"How do you do, Your Majesty! What can I do for you?"

"Answer the questions our guests put forth!" said the king. Avanti readily lent his ear to the questions.

One of the guests asked: "The earth has a navel. Where is it?"

Without hesitation, Avanti pointed with his stick: "Right there, on the piece of ground under my donkey's right front leg."

"How do you know it's right there?" The guest's manner changed with his amazement over the prompt reply.

"If you don't believe me, go and measure it for yourself! If it's even a hair's breadth out of place, you can come back to ask me again!" was Avanti's reply. The guest had nothing more to say, so he stepped quietly aside.

Avanti then asked the second guest to come forth with his question, which was: "How many stars are there in the sky?"

"Count the hairs on my donkey's back and you'll know how many stars there are in the sky," Avanti answered.

"How can you prove that?" the guest asked, trying to confound him.

"If you don't believe me, you can go and count the hairs of my donkey one by one. If there's one hair more or one hair less, come and ask again!"

"How can you possibly count the hairs on your donkey's back?"

"Now you are smartening up a bit!" Avanti said. "How can you possibly know how many stars there are in the sky!"

At this, the second guest also lapsed into silence. Avanti waited for the third guest to ask his question.

"You see the beard I have — tell me the number of hairs in it!"

"If you tell me how many hairs there are in my donkey's tail, I'll tell you how many hairs there are in your beard!" Avanti replied. Thus, the third guest also had to give up and admit defeat.

The Price of a Fowl

There was a porter who one day had fowl for dinner at an inn. When he asked for the bill, the innkeeper said: "If you are short of money now, you can pay me later. I'll write it up for you." Overjoyed, the porter thought this was the first time that he had met such a kind-hearted man. So he thanked him and departed.

After some time, the porter came to clear his debt. The innkeeper began figuring out the sum by putting one copper coin after another on the table, as if it were a complicated problem. Impatiently the porter asked: "How much was that hen of yours, after all? Surely you can tell me! Why do you make such a fuss about it?" The restaurant owner waved his hand as a sign that he did not want to be disturbed in his calculation. Since there was nothing else to do, the porter sat down waiting.

At long last the innkeeper had made out the account — the porter learned to his shock that he was supposed to pay for the fowl a sum several hundred times higher than the ordinary market price! He asked: "How can a single hen cost so much?" "Why not?" retorted the innkeeper. "Figure it out for yourself! If you hadn't eaten up that hen, how many eggs couldn't she have laid? And the eggs would have become laying hens again and they would have grown up to lay eggs. . . ." So grumbling, the innkeeper again put a great number of coppers on the table and said to the porter: "Look, that's the price — not one copper less!" The porter could not stand this any longer. "You aren't doing business, you're swindling people!" he shouted. "I won't give you the money!"

When the innkeeper saw that the porter would not yield, he condescended: "Let's go to the mosque then, to get the matter settled!" Sure of his right, the porter declared: "If you are in the right you can go round the whole world; if you're in the wrong, you can't move an inch. Even if you go to Allah, not to say to the mosque, you still have to speak within reason!" Pulling and dragging at each other, they came to the mosque.

The Imam of the mosque not only had charge of religious affairs; he was also the authority in legal matters and his word was law to the Moslems of his community. When the innkeeper and the porter came in, he was sitting on his carpet chewing tobacco. His side-whiskers looked like pieces of felt sticking to his cheeks. Since he chewed tobacco all day long, people said of him mockingly that his whiskers were so strong because the tobacco acted as fertilizer. Casting a sidelong glance at the two men, he asked in a slow, harsh voice what the matter was.

The innkeeper first gave his version and the Imam thought it quite reasonable. So he pronounced judgement even before he let the porter speak, merely telling him to pay the amount demanded by his creditor. The porter realized that arguing would be of no use; he only asked to be allowed to pay up a few days later. To that the Imam agreed.

Full of his grievance, the porter dragged himself home. Suddenly he heard a voice singing and a man riding a donkey was coming towards him. When the man came near, he put his right hand to his chest, made a respectful bow and said: "Brother porter, how are you?" The sight of this carefree fellow annoyed the sorrow-laden porter even more. His only response was "humph" before he hurried on. The donkey-rider was taken aback. He immediately turned his donkey round and caught up with the porter. "Brother porter, why are you in such a hurry?" he inquired. "What makes you feel so blue? Can't I be of any help to you?"

The porter stopped short and asked curiously: "Who are you?" "I am Nasrdin Avanti," the man on the donkey replied. At that, the porter was beside himself with joy. "Oh, so you are the famous Nasrdin!" Like everybody else, the porter had heard about Nasrdin, the man who went from place to place speaking up for the poor. In this case, too, Nasrdin was the man straightforward and sincere that people knew him to be.

The porter poured out all the details of what had happened. After a while, Nasrdin said: "Go right back to the mosque and say the judgement is not fair! Ask the Imam to hold a public trial. I'll take your case, don't worry!" The porter returned to the mosque at once. The Imam could not but consent, as it was a common practice that anyone could ask for a public trial. But if the accused were to lose again, he would receive double punishment.

On the day of the public trial the jury came to the mosque amid crowds of people. After the Imam had declared the court open, the innkeeper again gave his side of the story. But when it was the porter's turn to speak, he kept silent. "Why don't you speak up?" asked the Imam. "My lawyer hasn't come yet," replied the porter. Then the Imam queried: "Who is your lawyer?" "Nasrdin," was the answer. On hearing this, the Imam and the jury were rather perplexed, but the people were very glad. They chatted in low tones among themselves, looking forward to some fun.

Nasrdin arrived only after a long while. Having saluted the people, he apologized to the Imam and the jury: "Excuse me for being late, but I had some important business to attend to." Trying to find fault with him, one of the jurymen asked: "Can there be anything more important than the case on hand?" "Yes indeed, there is!" said Avanti. "Just think of it for a moment. I'm going to sow wheat tomorrow, but the wheat seeds weren't roasted yet. Could there be anything more urgent than that? The reason why I'm late is that I had to roast three bushels of wheat seeds before I could come here."

The Imam and the jury were very pleased to hear such foolish talk and yelled, almost in unison: "That's all nonsense! Can roasted wheat seeds grow?" They shouted in order to get rid of Avanti as the lawyer, so that they could handle the case as they pleased. The people watching began to worry that Avanti might really be disqualified, if he did not answer properly. But Avanti spoke up with complete ease after the noise had died down: "You are quite right — wheat seeds that are roasted cannot grow. Then I want to ask you: how can a fowl lay eggs after it's been eaten?" The Imam and the jury were dumbfounded and realized that Avanti had meant to trap them by being late and saying silly things. The people were overjoyed and shouted: "That's right, how can a fowl lay eggs after it's been eaten?" Thus questioned by the people, the Imam and the jurymen had to cancel the earlier verdict and let the porter pay for the fowl he had eaten according to the market price. And thus the case was closed.

The Pot Bears a Son

Once Nasrdin Avanti borrowed a big iron pot from a rich man who was known to be very stingy. The neighbours even wondered why he should be so kind to Avanti. In fact he was not a bit kind — he let Avanti borrow his pot as if he were making him a loan.

After some time, Avanti came to the rich man and addressed him cheerfully: "Congratulations to you! Congratulations to you!"

"What for?" asked his creditor.

"Your big pot has given birth to a son," declared Avanti. "Isn't this a piece of good news?"

"Nonsense!" retorted the stingy man. "How can a pot give birth to a son?"

"If you don't believe me," replied Avanti, "just look — what's this?"

And Nasrdin untied a woollen cloth and brought out a small iron pot. No matter how serious Nasrdin looked, the rich man would not believe him. But then he thought to himself: "If Avanti is such a fool, it would be silly of me not to take advantage of him." So he acted out his delight at his pot having

had a son, and loudly echoed Nasrdin's admiration of this splendid occasion.

As Nasrdin carefully put the small iron pot into his creditor's hand, he said once more: "What a handsome son!" "Yes, yes," responded the rich man, "the little fellow really looks quite a bit like his mother." He looked at the pot again and again, sighed with admiration and then put it away. When Nasrdin took leave, the rich man said to him: "Take good care of my big iron pot from now on, may it have more sons like this one!"

After some time Nasrdin paid another visit to the rich man and said mournfully: "I've come to express my condolences to you!"

"What's happened?" the man asked in surprise.

"Your big pot is dead," said Nasrdin.

"Nonsense!" shouted the rich man. "How can a pot die?"

Then Nasrdin spoke up: "If the big pot can give birth to a son, why can't it die?"

All of a sudden, it dawned upon the rich man that it was he, after all, who had been fooled, that Nasrdin had played this trick on him very cleverly. Naturally he did not feel like letting Nasrdin have the big pot just like that, so he said: "Well, since my big pot is dead, would you be kind enough to send its corpse back to me?"

"I've already buried it," said Nasrdin.

"Where did you bury it?" the rich man demanded to know.

"In the blacksmith's forge," was the answer.

The money-lender could no longer contain his anger. "You swindler!" he shouted at Nasrdin. "You just want to rob me of my big pot!"

"It was you who robbed me of my small pot first . . ." said Nasrdin.

This started a quarrel, but in the end the rich man was ready for a compromise, for fear of arousing his neighbours and ruining his reputation. If Nasrdin would say nothing of the small pot, the big pot would be given to him. But unexpectedly Nasrdin refused this offer and kept on making a fuss until a big crowd of people had collected around them. Then, with a disdainful flip of his sleeves, he drew away. His purpose — to expose the money-lender's stinginess to public ridicule — had been achieved.

Buying Oil

Everybody thought of Nasrdin as the most brilliant man in the world, but his wife insisted he was a fool. One day, the neighbours took this matter up with her. "You always say that he is a fool. Tell us, then, what foolish things has he done?"

"There are too many," she said. "I'll give you just one example to convince you."

"If you really can," the neighbours said, "we shall admit you're right."

"I'm sure you'll share my opinion when I'm through," the wife said.

Then she told them of something that had happened only a few days earlier.

"Nasrdin had come back from a long journey. When he stepped into the house, I gave him a dressing down for being such a chattering magpie and staying away all that time. As you all know, Nasrdin is like a tiger in the presence of wealthy people, but with me he behaves like a timid sheep. Despite my reproaches, he made me a low bow and asked for Heaven's blessings, as if I were a stranger. Then he smiled at me: 'My beloved little skylark, aren't I back now?' All my anger vanished at that. Like a real skylark, I flew into his open arms. I closed my eyes and thought to myself: 'How lucky I am that Allah bestowed such a good husband upon me!' But in a short while he once again made me angry. He bethought himself of a business deal somebody had entrusted to him and became so engrossed that he murmured to himself about it and never heard a word of what I said. I knew this as a bad omen — he would soon fly off again. So I thrust a bowl and a string of cash into his hand and told him to go and buy some oil, since there was not a drop left. I just wanted to distract him, so as to keep him from going away again. But all the way to the oil-shop he was thinking about that business deal and he didn't even notice it when the shopkeeper poured oil into the bowl in his hands. Soon the bowl was filled to overflowing. The owner of the oil-shop asked him: 'Where shall I put the rest of the oil?' Since my husband had no other vessel with him, he turned the bowl in his hand upside down and said: 'Just pour it here!' and pointed at the small space formed by the rim at the bottom. The people round the store roared with laughter as the oil spilled all over the ground. Still absent-minded, Nasrdin kept pointing and muttering: 'Pour it, pour it!' The shopkeeper did as he was told. When Nasrdin came home with such a small quantity of oil, I asked him in amazement: 'How could these few drops cost all the money I gave you?' His reply was: 'There's more on the other side.' So saying, he turned the bowl over once again, and spilled the last bit of oil on the ground. . . ."

The neighbours split their sides with laughter till the tears came. Nasrdin's wife felt this was the